P9-CPX-492

P. S. 309 B'KLYN.
LIBRARY

The Heart Calls Home

Also by Joyce Hansen

Which Way Freedom
Out from This Place

The Heart
Calls Home

Joyce Hansen

Walker & Company
New York

Copyright © 1999 by Joyce Hansen

All rights reserved. No part of this book may be
reproduced or transmitted in any form or by any means,
electronic or mechanical, including photocopying,
recording, or by any information storage and retrieval
system, without permission in writing from the Publisher.

All the characters and events portrayed in
this work are fictitious.

First published in the United States of America in 1999
by Walker Publishing Company, Inc.

Published simultaneously in Canada by Fitzhenry and
Whiteside, Markham, Ontario L3R 4T8

Library of Congress Cataloging-in-Publication Data
Hansen, Joyce.
The heart calls home / Joyce Hansen.
p. cm.
Sequel to: Out from this place.
Summary: After the Civil War, former slave Obi Booker tries to
make a new life on a South Carolina island while waiting to be
joined by his beloved Easter, who is studying in the North.
ISBN 0-8027-8636-7
1. Afro-Americans Juvenile fiction.   2. Reconstruction Juvenile
fiction.   3. United States—History—1865–1898 Juvenile fiction.
[1. Afro-Americans Fiction.   2. Reconstruction Fiction.   3. United
States—History—1865–1898 Fiction.   4. Islands Fiction.   5. South
Carolina Fiction.]   I. Title.
PZ7.H19825He   1999
[Fic]—dc21   99-19596
CIP

BOOK DESIGN BY JENNIFER ANN DADDIO

Printed in the United States of America

2   4   6   8   10   9   7   5   3   1

To Dr. Harriet Pitts—a dedicated teacher—
a faithful friend

Author's Note

The Reconstruction era after the Civil War forms the backdrop for this story. While all of the characters are fictional, some of the incidents that touched their lives are based upon actual events.

This was a time of hope for four million freed people of African descent. Freed men and women were able to work for wages, enter contracts, send their children to school, and in some cases purchase land and begin to build their own communities, similar to my fictional New Canaan. When the Fourteenth Amendment was ratified in 1868, black men gained the right to vote, and black citizens were supposed to have equal protection under the law. By 1869 black men began to participate in the political process.

These were also dangerous and bitter times. Reconstruction witnessed the rise of the Ku Klux Klan, the Red Shirts, the Knights of the White Camellia, and other hate groups. These groups sought by fear and intimidation to keep blacks from voting and participating in politics and in other arenas of public life as full American citizens. Benjamin Randolph, a black senator from Orangeburg, South Carolina, murdered in October 1868 while campaigning for the Republican party, was but one of many blacks who were either killed or beaten during and after the Reconstruction era. In 1866 a black settlement in Pine Bluff, Arkansas, was burned to the ground, and all of the men, women, and children living there were hanged. There were also bloody riots in large southern cities such as Memphis, Tennessee, and New Orleans, Louisiana. White northerners who were active in Republican politics in the South were victims of violence as well.

The Reconstruction era ended in 1877 when the last of the federal troops were removed, and the political gains made by the freedmen were eradicated. Their determined and brave quest for freedom and full citizenship did not end, however, with that first generation of freed men and women. Their spirit breathed courage into the hearts of a new generation of children, women, and men who fought for full civil rights for all Americans.

The Heart Calls Home

Prologue

June 1866

Obi immediately recognized the dirt road leading to the Jennings farm.

"Driver," he shouted over the rattling horse and buggy, "let me off here." He practically jumped out of the carriage before the coachman halted the horses. He handed the driver two dollars and a generous fifty-cent tip for the ride from Charleston.

"Thank you, sir." The man tipped his hat, revealing a full head of thick gray hair. "This be your final stop, or do you want me to come back for you?"

"I'm returning to Charleston, but I don't know how long I'll be here. You best not bother about coming back. I'll hail a carriage along the road or walk."

The coachman stared admiringly at Obi, who wore his blue army uniform with his soft forage cap turned very slightly to the side. With his high cheekbones, deep-set dark eyes, and a surprising smile showing perfect white teeth, Obi cut a handsome figure. "You might have to walk back then," the man said, " 'less a black driver come by. White drivers won't pick up colored, especially soldiers. I know you a military man and all, but it dangerous walking these roads alone at night."

Obi shaded his eyes from the bright morning sun and gazed at the beginning of the pine forest in the distance and the nearby oak grove. Slowly the scene sharpened in his mind and became familiar to him once again. He reached in his pocket and handed the man another dollar. "Wait for me here," he said. "I'll be back in an hour."

"Yes, sir. Thank you, sir. I'll be right here."

Obi tried to remain calm as he strolled slowly down the path he'd often walked as a barefoot boy and a barefoot young man—the slave of John Jennings. Though he was wearing sturdy boots, he imagined that he could still feel the sandy soil between his toes. Now he was a free man, an army man, Corporal Obidiah Booker of the 104th U.S. Colored Infantry, assigned to the Freedmen's Bureau in Beaufort.

This was his second two-day pass since returning home to South Carolina from Tennessee in March, and once again he was using his free time to search for Easter and Jason, who had been slaves with him on the Jennings farm. Though they were not related by blood, they were the only family Obi had. And blood could not have made the need to find them any stronger.

Five years ago, leaving Jason behind, Obi and Easter had escaped from the Jennings farm near Charleston, South Carolina, and headed for the Union-controlled Sea Islands. On the way they were captured by Confederate soldiers and forced to work in a Confederate army camp. When Obi eventually escaped to join the Union Army, he left alone. Easter, determined to go back to the farm and get Jason, had refused to leave with him.

Although the war kept them apart, Easter lived in the center of his thoughts. He could not forget how she had felt in his arms when he kissed her good-bye before leaving the camp. Now they could become a real family. They were free to marry, if she would be his wife, and

Jason could live with them as their son. Someday, perhaps, he and Easter would have children of their own.

When they parted, he'd promised to return for her, and she'd promised to wait for him. He'd kept that promise last month, when he visited the old Confederate camp, which became a freedmen's settlement after the war. But she wasn't there. No one in the settlement knew her. The old slave couple, Mariah and Gabriel, who'd helped him and Easter while they were in the camp, had both died. Since Easter wasn't there, he guessed she'd returned to the Jennings farm.

As he continued down the familiar path and saw in the distance the rough split-rail fence that marked off the beginning of the Jennings's tobacco fields and the little log cabin where his old friend Buka had lived, Obi's heart raced in spite of himself. He couldn't control the rush of excitement that filled every pore when he thought about her.

How did she look now? Did she still have the same small, brown, heart-shaped face and lively eyes that closed and seemed to curl at the corners when she laughed? He guessed she'd be about eighteen or nineteen years old, since he was twenty-one or twenty-two. Neither one of them knew their exact age, because they'd both been sold to John and Martha Jennings as children. Jason, however, was now twelve years old. He'd been born on the farm, and his birthdate had been noted and remembered.

Obi picked up his pace when he reached the tobacco fields and saw in the distance the frame house and the nearby barn where he used to sleep. The fields were choked with weeds, and as he drew nearer to the Jennings's home, he saw that the roof of the once neat frame house sagged in the middle, and the weather-beaten shutters barely hung on their hinges. He saw neither hound, cow, mule, nor horse. Even before he knocked, he knew that no one would answer.

He tried the door, but it was locked. He then ran to the back of the house and banged on that door, knowing how senseless this was.

He looked up at the broken bedroom window. "Easter! Jason!" he yelled and banged on the door. The only response was the sudden flutter of several small brown birds.

Obi couldn't bear to look around him. Too many memories— Easter calling him to dinner, Jason running and singing. He rushed away from the house, and Corporal Obidiah Booker was almost forgotten. He was Obi again, racing through the Jennings's empty fields, heading deeper into his slave past. He ran toward the Phillips plantation. Perhaps Easter and Jason were working there. Maybe the Jennings family had moved west, as they'd said they would.

As he passed the creek that separated the Jenningses' small tobacco farm from the much larger Phillips plantation, he tried not to give in to the despair he'd felt when he didn't find Easter waiting for him at the camp. Where else would Easter and Jason be? Where else could they go? he wondered as he picked his way through the overgrown brush.

War had not touched the still-gleaming white columns of the Big House, and the cotton fields were still dotted with laborers, just as he remembered. He tried to return to the present, straightened his back, and started to march smartly up to the front door. Obi couldn't scale, however, the invisible wall of times past. Instead, he walked around to the back of the house as he'd always done when he and Easter were hired out by John Jennings to work at the plantation, or when he went there to deliver the tobacco that Jennings sold to Mr. Phillips. He walked toward the kitchen, separate from the rest of the house. He was hopeful that the cook, or her helper, Rose, was there.

Nothing else had seemed to change. Elderly women sat in front of cabins, watching young children. He was disappointed, though, when he looked into the kitchen shed and saw neither the cook nor Rose.

"Morning, ladies. Excuse me."

The younger woman was sweeping, and the other one kneading

dough. They both stopped what they were doing. The young one curtsied. "Oh, a soldier man. How do, sir?"

The older woman nodded. "Can we help you?"

"I looking for a girl name Easter."

"We don't know anyone use to be here," the woman said. "Me and my daughter work for the Phillips family since last year."

"She didn't live here. She live over yonder on the Jennings place."

"No one live there."

"You never hear tell of a girl name Easter or a skinny little boy name Jason?"

"Can't say that we do. We only hear from one of the old women who still live here after freedom, that all of the people who used to be here run away."

"Who is this woman?"

"Would you like some clabber?" the younger woman asked, batting her eyes in Obi's direction.

"No, miss." He turned to the woman. "Do you know where I can find this old woman?"

"She dead," the woman answered.

"Are any of the other people who always live here still around?"

"No, sir, they all die out. Like I say, the people who use to live here left. The old man, Mr. Phillips, he dead too."

He tried to control the throbbing in his head. "What about his wife?"

"She here. Maybe she know about them people you looking for."

Obi thanked them.

"You live around here?" the younger one asked.

"Gal, you too forward," Obi heard the older woman say as he dashed out of the kitchen.

He rushed to the front of the house and ran up the steps two at a time, forgetting his shyness about knocking at the front door. He knocked several times before a very young girl, no more than ten, answered, wearing a plain homespun dress and a little white apron. He almost said, is your mistress home? He caught himself, asking, "Is Mrs. Phillips home?"

"Yes. Is you a soldier? A Yankee?"

"Just tell her Obi would like to speak with her. She knows who I am. I'll wait right here."

The girl slammed the door, and he heard her screeching, "Anobi is here to see you, Missy. Anobi is here. He a soldier."

A few moments later, Mrs. Phillips came to the door. Her smile turned to a frown when she saw who "Anobi" really was. She seemed thinner and shorter than he remembered her. She squinted at him.

"What do you want here?" she shouted. "Your master and mistress were good to you. That poor Martha grieved herself to an early grave over you and that little wench you run away with."

The heat rose from Obi's feet to his head. "Miss, I just want to—"

"Look at you, a Yankee nigger soldier, come back to make trouble." Her white wispy hair fluttered around her head. She turned to the girl. "You run right now to Master George and tell him to come here with his shotgun. Tell him a Yankee soldier is here trying to kill your mistress." The girl hesitated. "Git, before I take a whip to you."

Before Obi could grab the girl, she'd already flown down the stairs.

"I just want to know where Easter is!" Obi shouted back at Mrs. Phillips.

"I don't know!" she screamed at him. "They didn't tell me where they were going when they ran away. If Easter shows back up here, she'll be arrested for kidnapping, because I know Jason would not have gone if it wasn't for her." The built-up anger and rage over her lost human property became so great, she began to tremble. "And as for Rayford and Rose and the rest of them who left us after we took such good care of them," she continued, "I'm having them arrested too. It killed my poor husband when they left us like that. Just killed him."

Obi's head throbbed. He backed away from her, overwhelmed by the urge to wring her little shriveled neck. He ran down the steps quickly before he lost his temper, and before the girl returned with a mob of vigilantes. Mrs. Phillips's shrill voice followed him. "You'll be swinging off a tree soon."

Obi did not take her threat lightly. Instead of walking along the open road that led to the path where the driver waited, he headed for the woods. As he began to pick his way through the brush, he heard a slight rustling near him and felt for his pistol. Suddenly, the same girl appeared from behind a honeysuckle bush. She looked frightened and was crying. "Mister soldier, I didn't tell them mens on you. I didn't see you trying to kill her. But she whip me if she find out I didn't go."

He relaxed. This girl wasn't so silly after all. "Don't cry. You walk real slow and you give Miss Phillips's message to this Mr. George. Tell him you saw me going that way." He pointed in the direction of the thick pine forest.

She quickly recovered. "Yes, mister soldier. You won't tell Missy?"

He shook his head. "You walk real slow."

He moved, as fast as he could, out of the tangle of branches and vines and brush as he made his way back to the road. Every nerve and muscle in his body was taut. His head was pounding, his mouth dry, and his whole being consumed by anger and disappointment. To his relief, the coachman had waited.

"Hello, sir," the driver said. "That wasn't long at all."

Obi nodded and quickly stepped into the carriage. The man could tell that he was disturbed. *Another one of them cases. Kin and love ones missing. Feel sorry for the young man. But that's the way things be now. Black people seeking each other all over the place.* He lashed the horses and the carriage rattled down the road.

Obi looked back at the path and the pines and oak grove beyond, and if he'd had a cannon, he told himself, he would have fired on the farm and the plantation and the entire surrounding area. Leveled it to the ground. Made it disappear from memory. Nothing had changed there, except that the people he knew and loved were gone.

He looked away, wanting to take his tortured head and bang it on the ground. He wanted to wail and scream the way a child would—but he was not a child, he was a man. So he held his aching head and tried to be manly, but he became a boy once more that day, consumed by the memory of his mother. She screamed, and he sobbed in the corner of a small ship that carried him from one of the Sea Islands to the South Carolina mainland—carried him away from her forever.

He sat in the corner of the carriage, grit his teeth, and swallowed his disappointment, anger, and bitterness. He was like a piece of stone all the way back to Charleston.

The coachman could feel Obi's sad and silent presence inside the carriage. He prayed for Obi. It didn't matter that he didn't know him.

Eventually Obi's headache subsided, replaced by a gnawing emptiness in his heart. That evening when he boarded the ferry that would take him back to his post in Beaufort, he vowed to find them no matter how many years it took.

Easter *had* returned for Jason. Perhaps they'd left with Rose and Rayford and the rest of the people from the plantation. She and Rose were close. Maybe they were among the thousands of freed people who were still flocking to the Sea Islands.

At least he knew that they were together. Easter would take good care of Jason. He'd find them; otherwise, he'd be locked forever in his slave past.

1

Besides soldiers the streets are full of the oddest . . .
children—dirty and ragged.

—*LETTERS AND DIARY OF LAURA M. TOWNE*

April 1868

Obi gazed at the long line of black men with a sprinkling of whites and could not shake the odd feeling that something special was going to happen that day. As usual, whenever Obi was in a new place, he searched for a familiar face—anyone who might give him information about Easter and Jason, or the people who had left the Phillips plantation. Fighting his shyness and distrust of people he didn't know, he even struck up conversations with strangers at times. These often ended up telling Obi their own stories of searching for a sister or brother, a mother or father, a lover, a friend.

In the two years since he'd visited the Jennings farm he had found out nothing. He'd gone back to the farm and the neighborhood surrounding the plantation. He'd also traveled to a few of the coastal islands—Parris, Port Royal, Ladies, Hilton Head—but there were many more that he had yet to step foot on. He promised to visit every one of them. Freed people were still pouring onto the islands, fleeing the beatings and lynchings and the hatred against them that was beginning to spread like a plague.

He carefully studied the faces of the men who were lining up at the courthouse so that they could vote. Perhaps this was his lucky day, and he'd find the one person who could lead him to Easter and Jason.

"We are witnessing history." Thomas startled Obi. "Black men have been given the right to vote," he added.

"Y'all be witnessing buckshots in your hindparts if you don't pay attention to these woods behind us," Peter said, his eyes roaming the slight rise of hills covered with pine and oak trees.

"Okay, Peter." Obi turned to several other men who were also from the 104th U.S. Colored Infantry, part of a small company of soldiers sent from Beaufort to guard the men voting for a new state constitution.

"Time for another round of patrols, men," Obi said. "Two of y'all go check that thicket. It don't look natural to me." Then he turned to Thomas and Peter. "Let's see what's over on the other side of the hill."

"Good spot for a sniper," Thomas muttered in his clipped northern accent as he rushed ahead of Obi and Peter.

Peter, large and husky, frowned at Obi. "Soon as I muster out of this army, I'm leaving the South. You still ain't free if you can't go and vote without soldiers guarding you. Let me tell you, the only reason the freed people ain't all been killed dead is 'cause the army and the Freedmen's Bureau still here. When they go—" He ran his index finger across his throat. "Death to all blacks and all Republicans—white ones too."

"Hush, Peter," Obi said. "Concentrate on what we doing here."

Obi watched the back of Thomas's large head bobbing up and down, and his nervous quick movements as he stomped through the brush, loudly crunching dried leaves and twigs. That city boy still scared of the woods, he mused. "Peter, make Thomas slow down. He sound like a herd of buffalo, someone hear him coming a mile away."

Suddenly, one of the soldiers who'd walked toward the thicket on the other side of the hill called out, "Corporal Booker. Over here."

Obi ran to him, with Peter and Thomas following. "My God," Thomas gasped.

Three frightened children were huddled in the thicket. Their feet were tied with filthy rags, and the eldest child wore a long shift so old and worn it seemed as though it would crumble at a touch, like yellowed parchment. The two younger children, one of them a toddler, wore dirty shirttails and were partially covered with a dirty blue blanket. Sores and scars covered their arms and legs.

Obi kneeled in front of the biggest girl, who appeared to be about ten years old. He couldn't tell whether the other two children were male or female. The girl cradled the toddler in her arms. The other child held on to the girl's ragged dress.

"You the only one taking care of these children?" Obi asked.

She nodded, staring at the ground.

"Where's your mama?"

"She dead," the girl answered in a leaden voice. "They all dead."

"Who? Your kin?"

"Everybody where we live. The white men come there. Pull everyone out the houses. Kill everybody."

"How you know everybody was killed?"

"They was hanging in the trees. Everybody. Miss Emma, Mr. George, Daniel, their boy used to play with us. Mr. Edward, Miss—"

Obi patted her shoulder and stopped the recital. The images her words created were clear enough. Her story was the worst he'd heard so far.

"Lord, lord, lord," one of the soldiers murmured.

Obi continued. "Where this happen?"

She still stared at the ground. "Pine Bluff."

"In South Carolina?"

"I don't know, sir."

"How you get away?"

"My mama and us hide in the woods. Then when the men leave

the next morning, we see everybody hanging. All of them. Miss Emma, Mr. George—"

"I'll get their names later. What happen to your mama?"

"We leave, and some white people help us. Carry us in a wagon. But my mama give out. She say though that we not from Pine Bluff. Say our home be in South Carolina. She tell us to go to the island. Our home is on the island."

"What island?"

"I don't know, sir."

"How you get here?"

"The white people give us to some black people and we walk and ride in boat and wagon with them. They leave us at the house down there." She raised her head slightly and pointed to the courthouse. "Say someone there help us. But we afraid and hide in the woods." She spoke in a flat monotone and stared at the ground again.

Why didn't she cry? Obi wondered. How could she tell this story so plainly and simply? He gently raised her chin so that he could look at her. Her eyes held an odd stare, as though she wasn't seeing him, even though she looked in his direction. He'd seen that same stare in the eyes of dying soldiers. She lowered her face as soon as Obi stood up.

"Have mercy," Peter mumbled.

"These your kin?" Obi asked her.

She nodded. He touched the baby's hand, burning with fever.

"This my sister, Araba."

"What's your name?"

"Grace. And that's my brother Scipio."

"You know your age?"

"Yes, my ma told me. I was born April 29, 1857. Scipio born December 17, 1863. And Araba, she born on February 3, 1867."

The boy's eyes were large and frightened as he searched the soldiers' faces while clinging to his sister.

"Hey, little fella," Thomas said, "everything's fine now." He rubbed the child's head.

"He's a handsome boy," Peter said, taking Scipio's hand.

They led the children down the hill, and Obi took them to a well behind the courthouse so that they could wipe their arms and faces. Obi and Peter pulled out their blanket rolls and let the children rest under a large shady oak near their post.

Peter took biscuits and fruit out of his haversack.

"When you last had something to eat?" Obi asked the girl.

"I don't remember, sir. We drink some water when the people leave us at the building over there. One other day ate some berries, sir."

The soldiers shared their rations with the children. "Don't give them too much," Obi warned them. "They get sick if you stuff them." Scipio's eyes gleamed when Thomas handed him a juicy plum. After they ate, they slept soundly and deeply. Obi checked a few times to make sure that they were still breathing. He didn't think the youngest child was going to survive, though. She was feverish and hadn't eaten anything.

Just before dusk, when the polls closed and the voting ended, Obi woke the children so that they could begin the seven-mile trip back to Beaufort with the soldiers. Peter, unusually quiet, shook his head as he watched the children. "This just the beginning. Now the fight is no longer brother against brother, but white against black."

"Maybe the girl exaggerates," Thomas said.

Obi and Peter glanced knowingly at each other. "You from the North and ain't never been a slave. You don't know how it is," Obi said. "I know that child speak the truth."

Obi lifted Grace and Araba onto his horse, while Scipio rode with Peter. The boy's eyes, no longer fearful, were wide with excitement.

The small detachment of soldiers followed Obi. Grace and Araba fell asleep in his arms as the mare trotted along at a steady pace. His mind wandered to Easter and Jason, never far from his thoughts. He hoped that they hadn't witnessed the kind of horror these children had seen. Maybe he should have taken Jason when he and Easter had run away. And if he had, perhaps they'd all be together now. He pushed the thought away and concentrated instead on the woods encircling the road leading back to Beaufort. Obi held the girls securely and quickened the mare's pace. That odd unsettling feeling he'd had all day that something special was going to happen might really be a warning of danger, he thought to himself.

However, something special *had* happened; Obi just didn't realize it as yet.

2

Twelve labors of Hercules faced the Freedmen's Bureau.
—*W. E. B. DU BOIS*, BLACK RECONSTRUCTION

It seemed as though Obi had just fallen asleep when he heard Thomas yelling in his ear, "Wake up, man, and go see about them children. I'll let the major know so he can file a report."

When they'd returned to headquarters the night before, Thomas had advised Obi to let the children sleep in one of the cabins that served as temporary shelters for the refugees. They weren't supposed to allow civilians to sleep in the house, but Obi insisted on bringing the children inside the large comfortable home on Bay Street that served as offices for the bureau and living quarters for the soldiers. Obi made space for them in a small storage room. "You stay here till I come get you in the morning. You be safe here," Obi had told them.

Obi rolled off his pallet. He, along with Thomas, Peter, and five other men of the 104th, slept on pallets on the floor of the spacious, airy room, once an elegant sitting room. "This the best floor I ever sleep on," Obi had said when he first saw their quarters back in 1866.

He dressed quickly and walked down the corridor to the room where he'd left the children. They still slept soundly on Obi's and Peter's blanket rolls. Obi woke them and led them down the long corridor and out of the back door to the water pump at the rear of the house.

Obi reached for Araba. "Let me take her. She's very sick." He wanted to let Miss Jeffries, the northern missionary who worked for the bureau, examine her. Grace held her sister tightly. Her distant eyes suddenly focused on him, glaring with determination. "No. I can't. Mama said we must all stay together."

Obi could have easily snatched the child from her, but he couldn't bring himself to do that. "Clean yourselves. There's a water pump behind that fence. I'll be right back," he called after them.

He then rushed back to the house and ran upstairs to the supply room, where barrels were filled with old dresses, trousers, and shirts, donated to the Freedmen's Bureau by northern missionary societies and churches. Quickly rummaging through the garments, he picked whatever seemed appropriate. He returned to the children and draped the clothing over the fence.

"When you done, put these clothes on, then sit down at the table near the kitchen shed."

"Yes, sir," Grace answered.

Obi got a glass of buttermilk from the cook for himself, and asked him to give the children breakfast when they came to the kitchen shed. As he walked from the kitchen down the cobblestone passageway that led to the front of the building, he heard the horn sound seven times, giving the signal for everyone to report to their posts.

Obi approached the iron gates that opened onto the street, and saw that the line was long. He knew that the moment he took his post in front of the large sign that read BUREAU OF FREEDMEN, REFUGEES AND ABANDONED LANDS, people would swarm around him. Every morning as he opened the gate he scanned their faces, always looking for a familiar countenance, listening for a familiar name.

He approached the throng of blacks and a few whites and wondered how some of them had found their way to the bureau. Many were crippled, sick, half clothed, and half starved.

Obi, standing erectly with his legs slightly spread apart, hushed everyone as they called out to him for help. "If you don't listen, you won't know where to go. When you walk inside, the first door to your left is for food rations; the door on your right is the office for people looking for relatives or for people who want to register their name so relatives can find them. The large middle room is for people who need clothing, blankets, and housing. If you need to see the major about work contracts, then go to the back, a soldier will direct you to the major's office."

As usual, when he finished, someone yelled out, "What you say?" Obi sighed and patiently repeated the directions. During the busy morning, Obi also directed the cook to give the children porridge and milk, and after they ate he took them to see Miss Jeffries. She cleaned their sores, cut their knotted hair, and rubbed ointment on their scalps for head lice. Obi rummaged through the barrels again, found several blankets, and made pallets for the children in a corner of the large room near the windows opening on to a veranda. They still seemed weary. "You all rest for a spell," he said. They lay down, holding on to one another. The girls' dresses were too large, and Scipio's trousers could have held one more little boy.

"Corporal Booker, I need to talk to you." Miss Jeffries pulled him aside. "I think the youngest child has malaria. And the others are weak and will be sick too if they aren't cared for properly." She sighed and shook her head. "I think they've been beaten as well. They have old bruises and thick welts on their backs, arms, and legs. Maybe we can send them to the Orphan House in Charleston on the next steamer. They're overcrowded, but they might find space." She gazed at Obi thoughtfully. "Maybe the oldest girl could earn her keep. She could be bound out to a family. I don't know about the baby. We have to pray for her."

"Can they rest here for a while?"

"Yes. And they can sleep in the school cabin tonight. It's clean and safe. Don't you worry, Corporal. They'll be fine."

Obi started to walk away, knowing that no one could take better care of them than Miss Jeffries. She called him back. "Corporal Booker?"

"Yes?"

"This is a kind thing you've done for these children."

"I didn't do anything so special. Would help any children I find starving in the woods, ma'am."

She folded her arms and smiled. "But, Corporal, I think you did something special. The little fellow chattered on and on to me about how you saved them, fed them, and bought them new clothes."

Obi laughed. "Guess the clothes new to him. He never see them before."

Later on that day when he was taking a group of people to the storeroom for rations, he decided to check on the children. As he left the room and a cluster of cabins, he heard a little voice calling him— "Cupple Booker, Cupple Booker." Scipio left a group of children he'd been playing with in front of the cabin used as a schoolhouse and raced toward Obi with a big glowing smile. Obi was suprised that after merely a few hours of care, the boy's eyes looked so lively and healthy. He rubbed Scipio's head. "Corporal," Obi gently corrected, "not 'cupple.'"

Obi and Scipio walked toward Grace, who sat on a small bench outside of the cabin, holding her sister. He thought she smiled, but then her eyes took on the strange faraway gaze.

"You all doing good?" Obi asked.

"Yes, sir," Grace said.

Obi peered at Araba and touched her forehead. She was still feverish.

"The lady give her some medicine."

"And Cupple Booker"—Scipio pulled Obi's jacket—"we take a wash in the tub and she rub something stink on us."

"Scipio, you hush now," Grace said. "She say it good for us."

Obi smiled. "That make you clean and cure them sores. You all be good now," he said as he walked away. Scipio started to follow, but Grace called him back. Then she said, "Thank you, sir."

As Obi returned to his post at the front of the house, he saw Thomas walking toward him, carrying an armload of papers. "I rather be guarding something than wading through all of this junk," Thomas complained.

"What is it?"

"Old bureau and army records from Hilton Head. Some of these go all the way back to 'sixty-three."

Obi peered over Thomas's shoulder. "I want to look through them."

"Read them tomorrow night. We're going to a Republican rally tonight at Captain Small's home. Find out about the election if they've finished counting votes," Thomas said as he raised one leg on the step and rested the papers on his knee.

"By that time they get lost or someone throw them away by mistake. I have to read them tonight. You and Peter tell me about the meeting."

Thomas was almost a head shorter than Obi, but with a broader and thicker body. "Obi, the future is looking good," he said, "and we're moving forward, but you're letting the past drive you backward. I'm sorry you lost the girl, but you need to put your mind on your future. Easter, Jason, all of that is your slave past. You picked a new last name for yourself—Booker. You need to pick a new life for yourself too."

Obi shook his head and partially closed his deep-set eyes. "I have to learn what happen to them, Thomas. I need to know whether they dead or alive. I have no life without them."

Thomas looked thoughtfully at his friend, not understanding Obi's obsession. "Obi, suppose Easter is married with a husband and children of her own. Suppose a family has adopted Jason. Suppose, God forbid, they are both dead."

"Then I dead too." Obi glared at Thomas. "I think about that all the time. But now I live to find them." He leaned over Thomas. "You never been a slave. My slave past be my present too."

Thomas wished he could help his good friend, who seemed to be growing more silent and alone with each passing day. "You couldn't help what happened to you in the past. You didn't have a chance or a choice." He tapped his forehead. "But you have some say-so over this part of your life." He stood up straight, adjusting the papers. "You need to free your mind now."

"You can never know what it feel like to be a slave, Thomas. You know your family. I don't want to hear the lecture again. You tell me what happen at the meeting. Put them papers in the office where I can find them."

When the bureau closed that evening and the last needy person was helped, Obi was so anxious to look over the records, he decided to go to the office and read a couple of pages before he ate supper. Under the light of an oil lamp, he thumbed through the pages and stopped at a list of names of people who'd registered with the bureau in 1865.

John Powell and Mercy Powell, lived in Savannah, Georgia. Present residence, Wentworth Street, opposite Grace Church in Charleston.

Information wanted of my husband, Anderson Walker. When last heard from, September 2nd, 1864, was at Athens, Georgia. His former owner was Ferdinand Phirwell. Send information to Lucy Walker, 430 King Street, Charleston, S.C.

Toney Johnson, presently residing at 624 Prince Street, Beaufort, S.C.

Virginia Robinson, presently residing at Port Royal, S.C. Contact her through Freedmen's Bureau, Hilton Head, S.C.

As he skimmed the names, Obi saw a group of entries from people living on the Sea Islands. He recalled that Grace said she came from an island. He might, he thought, as he searched for Easter and Jason, come across an entry where someone was looking for three children. He came to the end of the 1865 list from the islands and found nothing; however, one entry caught his eye.

Esther and Jacob Jenkins, presently residing at New Canaan, Santa Elena Island, S.C., contact General Store, New Canaan.

Though he was tired and his eyes were beginning to burn, after reading a few other names, he went back to the Esther and Jacob Jenkins entry.

He'd been to Santa Elena Island. It was close to Beaufort and one of the first islands he visited. He found out nothing and hadn't heard of New Canaan. But there were many little villages that he hadn't heard of. He read the entry for the second and third times. Esther and Jacob Jenkins. Was it possible that someone wrote her and Jason's name wrong? It would be an easy mistake to make. Esther instead of Easter. Jacob instead of Jason. Jenkins instead of Jennings, their former master's last name. And knowing Easter, she'd choose Jennings for a last name. Often the Yankees had trouble understanding their speech. He tried to dismiss the entry again, but he couldn't ignore it.

He copied the information before putting out the lamp and leaving the office. After he ate, he'd come back and look through more of the pile. He had leave time next month and would go to Santa Elena Island again and find New Canaan. It was probably merely a coincidence that the names were so similar, but he had to be sure. He'd always had the feeling that Easter and Jason were on one of the islands.

3

*"Every mother's son among them seemed to be in search
of his mother; every mother in search of her children.*
—*FREEDMEN'S BUREAU AGENT FROM*
BEEN IN THE STORM SO LONG

May 1868

The driving rain was like a wall, and Obi couldn't see much beyond
the dock at Bay Street as the ferry pulled away. He found shelter under
a tarpaulin and managed to keep dry. He was glad to be alone, with
time to think. His days had been full and busy, and the children he'd
helped were still at the bureau. Miss Jeffries had told him she expected
to have a placement for them soon. Major Delany had found out that
Grace's story was true. A freedmen's settlement had been burned to
the ground in Pine Bluff, Arkansas, six months ago, and twenty-four
men, women, and children were hanged from the trees surrounding
their burned cabins.

Obi hated to think about it. Each time he saw Grace, however, her
faraway gaze, her unsmiling face, and her grim silence reminded him
of the horror she'd witnessed and of his own loss and longing.

By the time the ferry reached Santa Elena, the rain had stopped,
but the sun was hidden behind a thick blanket of clouds. As soon as he

stepped off the boat, he was greeted with smiles from the fishermen, stevedores, and others working on the dock.

"Happy to see you, soldier," an old man with a toothless grin greeted him.

"Hello, Father," Obi said respectfully. "Can you tell me where is New Canaan on this island?"

"Yes, mister soldier. That's the colored village where the people own their land."

"Is it far from here?"

"No, not so far. Just yonder," he said, pointing to the largest oak tree Obi had ever seen.

As Obi walked past the massive oak, its spreading branches reminded him of open, welcoming arms. He followed the shelled road into the freedmen's village and felt something different about the place. Maybe it was the way the tops of the trees met, forming a natural canopy over the winding path. Or perhaps it was the oak trees, thick gray moss dripping from their branches, standing near a cluster of cabins with their doors and shutters painted blue to keep away the haints and bad spirits.

When the shelled road turned into a dirt path, he saw a small frame building and guessed that it was a praise house, where the islanders held their weekly shout. Beyond the homes he saw cotton and corn fields dotted with men and women. Cabins stood at the edge of the fields.

Obi walked a few more feet and was relieved to see a store; adjacent to the store, a church was nestled in a grove of oak trees. Several cabins stood behind the church. An old woman sat on the porch of the store. Her bent fingers moved nimbly as she made a basket out of sweet grass.

"How do," the woman greeted him. "Who you seeking?"

"Is this New Canaan, Mother?"

"Yes. This be the place."

Obi nodded and smiled pleasantly at the woman. "I'm looking for a girl and a boy, Easter and Jason. Maybe people call her Easter Jenkins." Then he gave his usual speech, describing them and giving her their approximate ages.

"Nobody here go by those names, but you know people been changing their names. Everybody had to find a last name when we was freed. My husband and I use our old master last name. Just in case some of our kin be looking for us. Wayne, my name is Mary Wayne, but everybody call me Miss Mary."

Suddenly Obi realized that Easter might have been looking for him, thinking he took the name Jennings.

"I don't know for sure who these people are you seeking, because my husband use to run the store and I took over when he die two month ago. But Brother Paul might know. He the preacher and know all the new people moving here. A passel of them come just a few month ago."

"Where this preacher?"

"In he field."

"Do you recall any people by the last name Phillips?"

"I think some of them first people who come here in the time of the Yankee man and the war go by that name."

"You know a woman name Rose?"

"Yes. Rose Sabay. She have a son. Her husband was kilt."

Was it the same Rose? Maybe she'd gotten married and had children. Obi's heart began to beat faster, but he didn't want to get his hopes soaring, only to come crashing down. There was more than one Phillips family who'd owned slaves.

"Where can I find these first people?"

"They all about, son. Most of them be working in their field. You just have to go one by one and ask."

And so he did. He walked under the burning sun from field to field. As the day wore on, his legs cramped and he tried hard not to limp.

He repeated the same speech until it became almost a litany. By the time he had covered the ten square miles that made up New Canaan, he was exhausted, the heat sapping all of his strength. Everyone he'd met knew of the people from the Phillips plantation—the people from the time of the Yankee and the war, they called them. Some of them were sharecropping elsewhere, even though they owned land in New Canaan. Others worked at the mine near Charleston. No one had heard of Easter or Jason, or Esther Jenkins. Many said they were new to the island.

He followed a narrow footpath and saw a small marsh where a man was growing rice. Beyond the rice marsh, Obi noticed a cabin. It caught his eye because the door and shutters were not painted blue like so many of the other cabins.

"Good day," the man said. And Obi immediately began his recitation. Suddenly the man interrupted him with a great bear hug. "It's you! Obi from the Jennings farm."

Obi looked confused.

"You don't remember me? Samuel. From the Phillips plantation."

The man's broad smiling face was vaguely familiar to Obi. "Yes. I remember. You was one of the hands." A great burst of joy filled his heart, his spirit. At last he'd found someone from the old place.

"That's right. You a soldier?"

"Yes. With the 104th Regiment. Samuel, is Rose here with Easter and Jason?"

Before Samuel could answer, a spindly-legged boy chasing a toddler darted from behind a clump of bushes. The young child ran toward a woman.

"Look who's here," Samuel shouted to her. "Another one of us been found."

Obi could not take his eyes off her. He knew her. He knew those large dark eyes. She walked as erectly as a soldier, while balancing a basket on her head and carrying a three-legged pot for cooking rice when working in the fields.

She stared at Obi too—as though she were trying to remember. Then suddenly she put her basket on the ground, spread her arms, and shouted, "My Lord, Obi. It really you?"

His name coming out of her mouth jogged his memory. It *was* Rose. She gathered him up in her soft, comfortable embrace.

She held him at arm's length, then hugged him close to her again. The toddler grabbed her skirt, while the older boy tried to pull him away. "Leave your mama be," the boy said.

Rose held his face in both of her hands. "Obi, I can't believe it's you. You a soldier?"

He nodded. His joy subsided somewhat, and his heart was fearful as he asked the question. "Rose, where Easter? She here with you?" He saw the answer in her great dark eyes before she spoke.

"She not here, Obi."

4

O still green water in a stagnant pool!
Love abandoned you and me alike.

—ARNA BONTEMPS

"You know where she is? She marry? Is she dead?" His voice cracked.

"No, bless God, she fine, and I don't suppose she'd marry no one but you. Easter in a school in Philadelphia."

Obi relaxed, though his heart raced and his temples pulsated.

"And Jason?"

"He with a traveling medicine show."

"Easter promise to wait for me at the place where I leave her. Now she even let Jason go?" His deep-set eyes looked pained. "I think of nothing nor no one but her and Jason all these years."

"She want to stay here, but Easter's a smart girl. She learn to read and write in our little school. The missionaries send her to a school up in the north. She try her best to find you, Obi, even went to the Freedmen's Bureau and register herself there."

"I find the notice by accident. Wasn't even sure it was her. If she waited like she promise, we would've been together from two years ago." He felt himself growing angry, and his head was beginning to pain him.

"Wasn't no accident. You wasn't meant to find her till now. She coming back, Obi. Come, I tell you everything." She picked up her basket, placing it on her head, and walked toward the cabin he'd seen in the distance.

"Miss Rose, I going back in the field."

"Yes, Simon. I'll be there directly." She turned to Obi. "That boy a good help to me. No mother, no father, so I take him in."

The child held onto his mother's skirt as they walked along. They entered a neat two-room cottage, the same home Obi had seen near the marsh. Rose motioned for him to sit at the pine table as she took a pitcher and a tin cup off the mantel and poured him a drink of water. The baby scrambled into Rose's lap when she sat down in front of Obi. She seemed thinner than he remembered her, not as round and plump. "Why you in the field, Rose? You can't find work as a cook?"

"These are *my* fields, Obi. I working for myself." She told him her story.

"Easter escape from the Confederate camp and come back to the Phillips plantation. She arrive just in time, for the next day we all escape the plantation. Rayford had it plan for a long time."

"Who leave?"

"A passel of us. Samuel, Melissa, Sarah, Elias, Isabel and Paul, Virginia and George and their sons, Nathan, David and Isaiah, James, Julius, me and Rayford. Julius been a soldier too. He a hardworking man and manage to buy up a good amount of land. He know all them Republicans in Beaufort. And spend a lot of time getting people to vote with the Republicans."

She continued her story. "We get here to this island and grow cotton for the Yankees on this same plantation land. They promise we can get the land to keep when the war over. Me and Rayford marry. A real wedding too. This here is our baby, little Rayford. The Yankees don't keep their promise, and they give the land back to the family who abandoned it when the war start. But here on this plantation, we say we not giving back this land that we work on."

Her eyes watered as she rocked Little Ray, who was falling asleep.

"Rayford was shot and killed when the Yankee soldiers come to take the land and Rayford, Julius, and all the men refuse to leave."

He was shocked. "You sure it was Yankee soldiers?"

"Yes. They was Yankee for sure. Said that the land had to go back to the Williams family. The president and the government was giving the land back to the rebels."

"I know most of the white Yankee soldiers didn't like us, but I didn't think they shoot civilians."

"We get some of the land in the end. The Williams family sold it to us. My Ray had to die, though."

"Rose, I sorry."

"It God's will." Her large, sorrowful eyes slowly brightened. "Obi, you is like a godsend. We need men like you in New Canaan. You home now."

"And Jason. Where is he?"

"He with Dr. Taylor's medicine show. They travel all about. He write Easter and say he's coming to visit us."

Obi sighed and rubbed his forehead as he stared at the spotless table. "I wish she stayed and waited for me. Why she let Jason run off with a medicine show?"

"Jason was bound and determined to go. Easter couldn't stop him." She gazed at him for a moment. "Obi, why you looking so sad? Easter will return in September. You as good as find her now. And you find your home too," she insisted. "You know you always been one of us, even though you and Easter live on the Jennings farm."

She leaned across the table, her eyes large and hopeful. "Listen, Obi, we find out that the Williams family still owe so much money for tax they might have to sell the rest of their land. We want to buy this whole plantation. Then we really have our own village. A lot of the people here be renting land or sharecropping for the Williams family." She threw her head back proudly and hugged Little Ray. "But twenty-five of us own our land. I has twenty acres and plant cotton and corn. The government promised that people who been working these lands will get first chance to buy, before anyone else."

He poured himself another drink of water. "You believe that? The government ain't giving away land."

"I know. I ain't like some of these people still talking about the government giving them forty acres and a mule. Things different now. Julius and the other men in New Canaan have a Republican club, and they watching them buckra in Beaufort. Know just what them whites be doing."

"Them men from the north grabbing up land so fast, make your head spin," Obi said.

"I know it. Nothing left for people like us unless we stick together," Rose said. "Stay here with us when you're done with the army and build a future for you and Easter in New Canaan. I give Easter two acres of land when she leave. Build a house on it for you and her. And when the rest of this land for sale, you buy more. Grow your own cotton, instead of growing it for someone else."

"Rose, I just find you all. I'm happy to know that Easter and Jason is alive. I can't think on all these things you telling me now. Suppose Easter don't want to marry, or to marry me?"

"Obi, I ain't no mind reader, but I know Easter don't want no one but you, and I don't think she want to be a unmarried schoolmarm all of her life."

"You know Easter's address?" he snapped, beginning to grow weary of all of the talk.

"Yes." She stood up, holding Little Ray, who had fallen asleep, and placed him on Simon's pallet. "I didn't mean to tell you what to do. Guess I forget that you and Easter is grown-up people. I just don't want you to take Easter away. We been like sisters."

"I didn't say I was taking her away, Rose."

She took a box off the mantel and removed a letter. "When Easter write a letter, Miss Fortune, the teacher, read it to me." She looked embarrassed. "Rayford started teaching me, but then he die. Now I have no time. Can you read?"

"Yes. I learn in the army."

"You can write to her then. You remember this box?"

Obi nodded. He remembered it well. It was Rayford's box where he'd hidden a pen, ink, and paper so that he could write passes; Rayford had written Obi a pass the night he and Easter ran away, using paper from that same box. Obi copied Easter's address, and then he and Rose were able to talk to each other. With the bright sun shining through the open shutters and door, and the sweet scent of the azalea bushes, they spoke of their old life—the people they knew, the times they'd lived through.

When Obi got up to leave, Rose said, "Obi, think about what I tell you. Easter be back here in a few months. You could start putting up your home and be living here when the land available for sale."

He wouldn't get angry with her again. She was determined to have her say. "I muster out of the army in July. I'll write you and let you know whether I go to Philadelphia, or wait here for Easter."

"I wish I could see the joy on Easter's face when she get your letter. Now, you write to me at the general store," she instructed. "Miss Mary will give me the letter, and the teacher will read it to me."

Obi had time on the trip back to Beaufort to organize the events of the day—to make them clear and orderly in his own mind. He still couldn't quite believe that he'd finally found out where Easter was. But he wouldn't be able to celebrate until she and Jason were at his side.

It seemed to Obi, however, that when the ship docked in Beaufort that evening the stars shone brighter than usual and the full moon cast a soft light on the harbor. As he walked along the dock and headed toward Bay Street, the air felt warm and soft like velvet.

When he reached headquarters, instead of going to the room he shared with the other men, he went to the office where the records were kept. He lit the lamp and found a pen, paper, and ink. Even though he had thought about all of the things he would say to Easter as he rode on the ferry, there were no words for the feelings so deep and strong in his heart. But he did the best he could.

May 20, 1868

Dear Easter,

At long last I find you. So many things happen since we part. I will tell you all when I see you. I'm in the Army, but will be out in July. Rose give me your address. I find her today. I been seeking you and Jason for these many years. Easter, I never ask you before, because you was just a girl when we parted. But the whole time we was separated I think of no one but you, and I begin to dream of a time when you and me become husband and wife. Easter, will you marry me? Do you want me to come and get you when I muster out of the Army in July? Or, do you like the life in the north? Easter please tell me what you want to do. I wait anxiously to hear your answer.

Also, other news to tell you. I been to the old confederate camp looking for you and find out Mariah and Gabriel both die back in 1866. Martha Jennings die too, or so Miss Phillips tell me when I went there looking for you, also in 1866. I go by the last name Booker. Please write me back soon to this address.

Corporal Obidiah Booker
104th United States Colored Troops
Headquarters Bureau Refugees, Freedmen
  and Abandoned Lands
Beaufort, S.C.

Love, your Obi

He folded the letter and put it away in his haversack. Tomorrow he'd send it out by post, and wait impatiently for her reply.

5

Yours is the face that I long to have near,
Yours is the face, my dear.

—*ANGELINA A. GRIMKE*

Obi could not get annoyed with Thomas and Peter the next morning
when they nagged him about missing another meeting of the Beaufort
Republican Club. Every time he thought of Easter reading his letter,
he'd burst into a big smile. Not his usual way.

"Hey, Obi," Thomas boomed loudly, "man, you should've been
with us at the meeting last night. Good thing we coming out this army
soon. I think they going to have another civil war."

"What happen?" Obi asked.

"Almost every black man who was a delegate to the constitutional
convention had his life threatened. One of them has a guard day and
night in front of his house," Thomas said.

Peter grimaced as he pulled on his boots. "That's why me and
Thomas and some of the other boys heading west when we muster
out. There be land out there and true freedom. I hear they giving away
land—two, three dollars an acre. Rich as you is, Obi, you could buy
thousands of acres."

"You better come on with us, Obi," Thomas said. "Start a real
new life. I know you have the first dollar you ever made in the army.

Take that money out of the bank and come with us, Corporal Green-backs."

Obi smiled at their teasing, as he stretched his arms. He didn't drink, smoke, or gamble and had managed to save most of his army pay. "I find my Easter. "

Thomas's eyes opened wide. "You found her? You actually found her?"

"She's living on the island?" Peter asked.

Obi told them the whole story.

"I rejoice for you, Obi, but after you marry her, what next?" Thomas asked.

"Buy land on the island, if that's where Easter wants to stay. Have our own children. Open my own business, maybe. I know the carpenter's trade."

"Every black man in the south know the carpenter trade," Peter said. "And suppose the girl don't want to marry your hide?"

Even Peter couldn't anger him. "Then I take my money out of the bank and come out West with you. Buy that land you always talking about."

Thomas suprised Obi. "Peter, we all have to find our own way. Leave him be."

Obi put on his jacket as he gazed out of the window at the magnolia tree, beginning to blooming.

"I'm happy for you," Thomas said.

"Thank you, Thomas. Peter be about right though. Now the question is will she marry me."

"At least you know that she and the boy are alive. Seems as though they found new lives for themselves. You must do the same if she doesn't want to marry you."

Obi's pronounced high cheekbones looked as though they'd been etched in black marble, and his eyes were intense as he stared at

Thomas. *Can't make him understand.* "Won't have no new life without them, but I'll keep on living."

When Obi took his post in front of the house, he saw Miss Jeffries running toward him, appearing flustered.

"Corporal Booker, why did you give those orders yesterday? We had a placement in Charleston for the children."

"Miss Jeffries, what're you talking about?"

"The children. The baby was going to be put in the Orphan House, and a very fine lady was willing to take in the two older ones."

"Miss Jeffries, I give no orders about them children. I left them in your care." He glanced at the line of people forming in front of the house.

"When I told the oldest girl they'd be leaving for a new home, she says that you told them not to go anywhere. She said they were staying with you."

Obi tried to look as serious and disturbed as Miss Jeffries, but he wanted to laugh. "Ma'am, I think that little girl hoodwink you." A smile hovered around his lips in spite of himself. "I told her no such thing. Send them out on the next transport to Charleston."

"It will be too late. The Orphan House stays full. And the lady can easily get other children."

"Miss Jeffries, something else will turn up. And there be plenty fine ladies from Charleston who miss their slaves and want to train little black children for servants."

"You're wrong, Corporal. This is a refined lady of color. Childless, who would be willing to train them and give them a loving home."

"Send her a letter and tell her the children will come with the next transport."

Miss Jeffries quickly walked away from him. He didn't blame her for being angry. Fooled by a child. In the meantime, nothing could spoil his almost good mood on such a perfect day.

In the afternoon, as fewer people trickled into the bureau, he left his post and walked over to the school cabin. He peeked inside. Grace sat quietly on a bench near the door. Araba was sound asleep, her head resting on Grace's lap. Scipio and two other children sat at a table and carefully wrote the letters of the alphabet on their slates. He didn't see Miss Jeffries, but Miss Caroline, the young black woman who helped her, was showing the children how to form their letters.

Obi entered the cabin, and the young woman smiled prettily at him. "Miss Caroline, can Grace come outside for a moment?"

She let Araba lie across the bench and walked outside with Obi.

"Why you lie to Miss Jeffries?"

"I didn't lie, sir."

"You lying now. You told her that I ordered you to remain here."

She stared at the ground. "I thought you want us to stay."

"How you think that?"

"When we was in the room, you say don't leave till you come get us."

"But that was in the room."

"I thought we couldn't leave here less you tell us to, sir."

This is a clever little girl, Obi thought. "Grace, you listen to Miss Jeffries and you go where she say. She's trying to help you all."

Grace kept her head lowered.

"Grace? You understand?"

"I thought we was staying with you, sir."

"You can't stay with me. Miss Jeffries will find a good home for you."

She kept her head lowered. "But we have to stay together."

"These missionary are good people. They won't separate you." He hoped that he was right. "Why ain't you copying your letters like the other children?"

"Can't see so good since that time."

"What time?"

"When they was hanging in the trees. Miss Emma and Mr.——"

Obi hushed her. "You could see before?"

"Yes, sir."

He lifted her chin. "Can you see my face?"

"Yes, sir."

"Then you can see."

"I only see your face. Nothing else. Can't see letters."

"But you can see my face?"

"Yes, sir. It cloudy though."

He looked at the top of her head and shook his own. This is a rock-hard, hardheaded little girl, he thought to himself.

"Grace, don't tell no more lies. Now you go on in there and learn your letters. When you was a slave child, it was against the law for you to get learning."

As he walked away though, he wondered. Perhaps there was something wrong? Later that day, he asked Miss Jeffries to examine Grace's eyes. "Now who's being hoodwinked, Corporal? I see nothing wrong with the child's eyes. And if there is, which I doubt, it could've been taken care of at the Orphan House."

Though his days were busy, each one felt like a year as Obi anxiously waited for Easter's reply. In the meantime, Miss Jeffries informed him that the fine colored lady from Charleston had taken in another child, and the Orphan House was full. The children remained at the bureau. And the days that stretched so long for Obi were like medicine for the children, as they grew stronger and healthier—even the frail Araba.

Obi saw them daily. Scipio made certain of that, searching out "Cupple Booker" to proudly show him how well he and Grace were writing their letters. Obi suspected, however, that Scipio was writing for Grace.

Finally, in the middle of June Easter's letter arrived. Obi didn't receive it until the early evening, the time for mail call. He rushed out of the office as soon as the clerk handed him the letter, not wanting Thomas and Peter asking him questions. He didn't know what Easter had said. Maybe she wasn't even planning to return to the South. Maybe that was just Rose's wishful thinking.

Obi left headquarters and walked to the docks. The sky was streaked with pink, red, and mauve, and as they always did, the cries of the seagulls reminded him of his mother and the way she screamed when he was taken from her. Obi found a deserted spot near a rotting, unused berth and steeled himself.

May 27, 1868

Dear Obi Booker,

Is it really you? My Obi from the Jennings farm? Why did you name yourself after the old African? All this time I thought that you took the name Jennings and I've been looking for you with that name. When I received your letter today I cried for joy and sorrow. I'm grieved that Mariah and Gabriel have died. She looked poorly when I visited her last. And Mistress Jennings, I know I shouldn't say Mistress, but it doesn't seem right saying anything else. Maybe it's not true that she's dead. Maybe Miss Phillips told you that to hurt and worry you. When I return I'm going to visit the old place and find out for certain whether it's true.

Obi, I cried for joy too, knowing that you are alive. Believe me I tried to find you. I went to the Freedmen's Bureau in Elenaville and Charleston.

I always remember how we kissed before you left the camp. But I think it's just a foolish young girl's thoughts, and that after all of

*this time you probably have a wife and children. Of course, I will
marry you. I have waited all these many years.*

*You asked me whether I want you to come to Philadelphia.
Since I received your letter I think about you all of the time. I see
your face between the covers of my school books when I should be
studying. I want to see you more than anything. However, I don't
think you should come here now. If you do, you will spend all the
money you save just to eat and rent a room. It is hard for the colored
people to get work and when they do it pays very little. Only a very
few live like the Fortunes. These northern buckra, bad as the ones
back home. I do not want to live in the North. The people can be as
cold as the weather. Santa Elena Island is my home and I rather
suffer southern rebels than some of these northern rascals.*

*I will be practice teaching at the orphanage for colored children
in July and August and will be home in September. It is not so
long, not as long as it has been.*

*Rose gave me two acres of land. Stay on it and build a house
for us and Jason and all of the beautiful children we will have.*

*Let me tell you about my new life. The best thing about living
in Philadelphia is the school and the Fortune family. They are the
most wonderful people. They are not like some of the colored people
I have met who think that they are better than people like us who
have been slaves. The family took me in and treat me well. I didn't
know that some colored families live almost as grand as the Phil-
lipses. The Fortunes have a maid and a woman who does their
laundry. I have to help them when I am done with school and my
studies, but I don't mind. I am earning my keep.*

*I love school very much, even though some of the other colored
girls who have always lived in the North make fun of me behind my
back. They laugh at my speech, though I try to talk Yankee style
when I am around them. But I ignore them because I am just as*

free as they are. The girls stop laughing when I learn Geography, Mathematics and History better than they do.

I have not heard from Jason for a while and I am beginning to worry about him. He hasn't written to me since April when he was in Georgia. I pray he's well and that Dr. Taylor is taking good care of him. Jason didn't leave an address because they were traveling. When I return Obi and we marry, the first thing we will do is bring that rascal home to be with us.

Give Rose and everyone my love. Please write me back soon. I cannot wait to hear from you again.

Love always,
Easter

Obi was overwhelmed. His dark eyes watered, and he could not control the tears of relief that glistened on his high cheekbones and ran down his thin face.

He read the letter three more times to make certain that she really said, Yes, she would marry him. Obi felt so foolish as he wiped his face that he had to laugh at himself. *Big stupid man crying.* He kissed the letter, folded it, and put it in his pocket. He felt as though he'd been tied up with great thick chains and was suddenly able to burst out of his fetters.

Obi hurried back to Bay Street, feeling as though he could jump and spin and fly with the gulls in celebration. No longer would the cries of the seagulls remind him of his mother's screams; from that time on they would be to him cries of pure joy. He answered Easter's letter that evening, telling her that he'd be waiting for her in New Canaan when she returned.

He flung his heart open, finally, unafraid to be happy.

6

*Major Delany was fully cognizant of the
exceeding delicacy of his position.*
—*FROM* LIFE OF MAJOR DELANY

July 1868

The air was heavy with moisture, while the sun fought to break through the thick clouds. Red myrtle bushes colored the yard. Obi smiled slightly at Scipio, Grace, and Araba. They solemnly watched the mustering-out ceremony. Miss Jeffries, Miss Caroline, and some of the other bureau employees watched too.

Obi felt a tinge of sadness as as he listened to Major Delany complete his farewell address. Delany was one of the few black officers in the Union Army, and the men of the 104th U.S. Colored Troops were proud of their commander. Not a crease was out of place in the major's uniform, and the saber hanging at his side gleamed like a jewel as his voice rang clearly across the yard.

"Congress has passed the Fourteenth Amendment, which states that all persons born in this nation are citizens. And that includes formerly enslaved people. Every citizen, no matter what his color, shall have equal protection under the law." He paused and stared intensely at each and every one of the men. "You men have been instrumental in making this amendment a reality. You have made the way easier for the generation that follows. Never let anyone treat you as less than a man. Acquire land and property, acquire learning, but most of all, acquire love. We have lived with hate too long."

Obi's throat tightened, and he lowered his head so that he could compose himself before facing Thomas and Peter. He wondered whether he'd ever see them again, and began to miss them already. The major shook everyone's hands and handed them their discharge papers.

"We're heading out now," Thomas said. "Soon as I get Peter away from that pretty little lady over there. I'll write you as soon as I can, so you know where to find us if you change your mind about going west."

While they both smiled at Peter, who was trying to catch Miss Caroline's eye, Scipio dashed over to Obi. "Congratulations, Cupple Booker!" he shouted, giving Obi a salute. With a smile almost as wide as Scipio's, Obi returned his salute.

Thomas rubbed Scipio's head. "I think we have a future army man here." Obi looked around and saw Grace shyly standing in the corner, with Araba in her arms. He'd learned this morning that a new group of refugees was being relocated to a work farm on Edisto Island run by missionaries, and the children were included. He would be sailing on the same ferry, which was stopping first at Santa Elena Island.

Miss Caroline called the children to take them back to the school, and Scipio turned to Obi. "Can I stay with you?"

"You go on. I'll be around to the school to see you."

"That little fellow looks like he's attached himself to you, Obi," Thomas said.

Obi nodded. "I hope the missionaries find them a good home on the island."

Peter walked over to Obi and Thomas. "We not saying good-bye," he announced. "We just saying see you in a while."

The three men hugged one another, and for a brief moment Obi regretted not going with them. It passed, though. He sadly watched them walk toward the house until they disappeared inside. Too many good-byes in one day. Suddenly he wanted to do something special for the children. He left the yard and pushed his way down Bay Street, toward the general store on the corner. The street was unusually crowded with vendors, sailors, refugees, and a few idlers.

He purchased a pink gingham dress for Grace and a linen shift and porcelain doll for Araba. And for Scipio, who was never without a smile and a warm greeting for everyone, especially "Cupple Booker," he bought a writing book and a pair of trousers. He also purchased a dainty beaded purse for Easter.

When he finished making his purchases, he walked across the street to the Freedmen's Savings and Loan Association. He withdrew the $500 he'd saved out of the $840 he'd made while in the army. He smiled to himself as he carefully put the money in his billfolder. He would give Easter, himself, and Jason a good home—something they'd never had.

Obi hurried back to headquarters and found the children standing in front of the house with a group of about thirty other men, women and children. Grace held Araba, and Scipio looked as though he had been crying. When he saw Obi walking toward him, however, he was transformed. "Cupple Booker," he shouted.

Obi handed Scipio the package. "Here some gifts for all of you. Don't lose this package, Scipio."

Scipio's bright eyes danced. "No, Cupple. I won't."

"Thank you, sir," Grace said softly.

He knelt in front of them as he'd done when they first met. "You going to a new home where you'll be safe. Maybe the missionaries find your kin for you. Your ma said you came from an island. Maybe you have kin where you're going."

Grace kept her face lowered as Obi spoke. He lifted her chin, and her eyes focused on him for a moment, then took on the faraway gaze. "You understand, Grace?"

He rubbed Araba's little hand, and she smiled. Her eyes were no longer glazed and feverish.

"You coming with us?" Scipio asked excitedly.

"I'm going on the ferry, but—"

Miss Jeffries rushed over to them. "Come now, children. You have to go with the others."

"But Cupple Booker, you coming too?" Fear was beginning to cloud Scipio's face.

"You go on with Miss Jeffries. Don't lose that package now." Scipio held Grace's hand and looked back sadly at Obi, his eyes swimming in tears. "Go on now." Obi could hardly look at them. "You act like a big boy now, and watch over your sisters."

When Obi boarded the ferry later on that morning, he found himself gazing at the crowd, but he didn't see the children among the passengers, and that was best. They had to grow accustomed to their new situation. They might get the idea that they were going with him.

Obi found a corner on the ferry and tried to relax during the two-hour trip to Santa Elena. He reached into his haversack and removed the letter he'd received from Easter a few days ago.

July 3, 1868

Dear Obi,

I hope this letter finds you well and happy. I suppose you will soon be going to New Canaan. I wish I were there to welcome you back to civilian life after bravely fighting for our freedom. But Sep-

*tember will be here soon and then we will have a grand celebration,
for we have much to celebrate. I began my practice teaching today
and assisted the principal teacher at the orphanage. Obi, I enjoyed
it so very much. The children appreciate every kindness we show
them. I think I will truly like this work. This is an orphanage for
colored children. Some of them are the children of freed men and
women, who left them in our care while they work, others are children who have always lived in Philadelphia.*

*This evening, Miss Fortune's sisters invited me to attend a mu-
sical recital with them and I had a fine time. The music and singing
were beautiful. The sisters treat me as though I were one of them,
but that is how the Fortunes are.*

*Please write me as soon as you reach New Canaan. This letter
is short, Obi, because the hour is late and I have to rise very early
tomorrow. When you see Rose, give her and all my friends in New
Canaan my love.*

Your Easter

As Obi read the letter and recalled the sound of Easter's voice, he
had no idea that a pair of bright little eyes were fastened on him during
the entire trip.

When the ferry docked, a crowd of people got off. Many of them
had been removed by the slaveholders who abandoned their plantations
when the Yankees occupied the territory in 1861. They were now returning as free people to family and friends and the only place they'd
ever lived. Some people were escaping the violence and persecution in
other parts of the state. He also saw a great number of black veterans,
like himself.

The passengers were noisy and happy as they waved at the crowd
on the dock. Besides the usual stevedores unloading the ferry, and the
vendors selling fruit and other produce, the dock was covered with

women and children waving small American flags. They had come to meet the returning veterans.

Leaving the ferry, he slowly pushed through the crowd and headed for the large oak that pointed the way to New Canaan. He'd sent Rose a note, letting her know when he was arriving. She might be in her fields, so he'd look for her there first.

Suddenly, he heard someone calling him excitedly and saw Rose rushing toward him with Little Ray in tow and Simon waving a small flag like the others. Rose embraced him.

"Rosie, you shouldn't take time from your work to meet me."

"I have to. All these soldier have someone here for them, Obi. Couldn't let you come home without a welcome too." Her eyes twinkled. "Easter wouldn't like that, you know. I tell everyone you coming here. You'll see them all tonight."

"Rosie, I told you, don't make a fuss."

"It's no fuss. We just so happy another one of us been found."

While Rose waved to several people, Little Ray kept turning around and pulling away from her. "Ray, what's wrong?" She turned around also, and then stopped. "Well, who is these little ones following us?" she asked.

Obi swung around and saw Scipio clutching the package he'd given him and Grace clutching Araba. Scipio's large brown eyes were bright and shining, while a guilty half smile played around his mouth.

7

Where you go I will go, and where you lodge I will lodge;
your people shall be my people.

—THE BOOK OF RUTH

"Why you get off the ferry? You all suppose to be going on to Edisto," Obi exclaimed angrily.

"I thought we was suppose to go with you." Scipio sniffled and bowed his head.

Obi knelt in front of them. "Grace, did you tell your brother that?"

"I thought so, sir. When Scipio say he see you leave, then we follow."

Obi stood up. "I never seen such determined children," he said to Rose. Even Araba smiled at him. "Come, you have to get back to the ferry," he said, taking Scipio's hand.

"We want to stay with you, sir; only you can help us. Please, sir, please let us stay with you," Grace's voice cracked slightly. For the first time since he'd met her, she sounded as if she would cry. "Please, sir. Please let us stay with you," she pleaded.

Scipio began to cry.

"You have to get back on the ferry," Obi said firmly, looking away from them. He began walking quickly, pulling Scipio and Grace along.

"Where they going?" Rose interrupted while Little Ray smiled at Scipio, and then started crying too.

"They're going to a work farm."

"I thought they'd be with kin."

"Please, sir. Please," Grace begged.

He gently pushed her forward. "Grace. I'm sorry. You can't stay with me. I have no home myself."

"Wait, Obi. We get someone here to keep them. People taking in children all the time." She pointed toward the dock. "Anyway, the ferry leaving. Y'all come on," she smiled at them. "You can stay with me for a spell."

"How can you take in three children?"

"I have plenty space. I'll make a pallet in my room for the girls to sleep on. The boy can sleep on a pallet in the front room with Simon. Unless he want to sleep in the shed with you."

"What shed?"

"Me and Simon clean the shed behind my cabin for you to stay in until you build your house. See, there be plenty room."

They walked past the store, and Miss Mary waved. "You find them children you was looking for, eh, Mr. Booker?"

He just smiled at her.

"These not his children, Miss Mary," Rose informed her. "She in your business already, Obi, and you just get here. If you want something found out, you just tell Miss Mary."

They passed the church surrounded by oak trees, and just before the shelled road turned into the footpath leading to Rose's cabin, he saw the praise house. Everything was familiar to him now—even the azalea bushes near the cabin and the large oak tree that towered over a small shed.

When they reached the cabin, Rose opened the door. "Come on in, everybody. Y'all sit. Girl, put that baby down. And get rid of that blanket."

"She can't walk, ma'am. She won't sleep without her blanket."

"I didn't know she couldn't walk," Obi said. "You never tell me, Grace."

Rose took Araba from Grace. "You never ask why she always carry the child?"

He was embarrassed. "I just thought it was her way of keeping the baby safe."

Rose rubbed Araba's thin legs. She turned to Grace. "Rubbing will strengthen these weak legs. You know how old she is?"

"A year, ma'am."

"Should be walking. She need fattening up."

Rose took the tin cups off the mantel and placed them on the table. "You know how to draw water?" she asked Scipio.

"Yes, ma'am."

She handed him a pitcher. "The well is near the shed back of the cabin. Get some water for your sisters."

Grace sat on the bench and gently rubbed Araba's legs.

Rose whispered to Obi as they stood by the door, "We can get them some help. Miss Fortune, the teacher, maybe can find a family who take them in. In the meantime they can stay here."

"I'll write a letter to the bureau and tell them what happened. Maybe I send them on the next army transport going to Edisto." He leaned close to Rose's ear. "I'll tell you their story later, " he whispered.

That evening, after the children were settled in, Rose insisted on taking Obi to the regular Friday-evening meeting of the New Canaan Republican Club. Rose left Simon in charge of all of the children.

"Everybody waiting to see you," Rose informed him as they walked down the shelled road. Before they reached the meeting, he told her about the children.

"My Lord," she gasped. "Seem cruel to throw them into a work farm. Just throwing them away again."

When they neared the church, she said, "This church be everything. We just have a little cabin for the school, so all the children's recitals are in the church, and it's the place for our meetings too."

The meeting hadn't begun as yet when they entered the small church. A few people milled around the back of the church; others talked quietly.

"Everybody, we find another one of us from the old place!" Rose announced loudly as she stepped down the narrow aisle that separated the rows of benches. Obi felt like disappearing as all eyes turned in his direction. He thought that he recognized a few familiar faces.

He heard someone say, "Obi from the Jennings place. You remember him."

Obi didn't recognize the stylish young man who walked over to him with an extended hand. He wasn't dressed like a farmer. His suit was made of fine broadcloth, and his shoes were shiny and new. "Obi, good to see you. You don't remember me? Julius."

Obi shook his hand. "Of course, I remember you. Just didn't recognize you." Julius looked nothing like the skinny ragamuffin he recalled.

"Welcome to New Canaan. You been in the army, I see."

"Yes. And you?"

"Oh, yes. Served in the Thirty-third. Made sergeant." He paused as if he didn't know what else to say. Then he asked, "Easter know you're back?"

Julius's words of welcome sounded empty, and he wondered why Julius hadn't even asked what regiment he'd served in. And why is he interested in what Easter knows? "We write each other," Obi replied.

"Well, that's very good." Julius abruptly walked away from him and greeted two white men who had entered the church. Obi wondered whether Julius was as important as he acted. When the two men were seated in the front row, Julius stood before everyone and brought the meeting to order. Obi leaned over and whispered to Rose, "Julius the boss man, yes?"

"He in this political thing with them Yankee Republicans."

One of the white men stood before the group. Obi immediately recognized his Yankee accent as the words raced out of his mouth. He talked to them about the new constitution that struck down laws restricting the freed men and women to field labor. He then congratulated Julius on becoming a member of the Land Commission.

"He really think he important now," Rose chuckled.

Julius bowed deeply and spoke next. "One of the most important thing this constitution give us is a system of common schools for all children, black and white," he exclaimed. "And the next important thing is the Land Commission. The commission make it easier for freedmen to buy the land. I know that the Williams family owe money for taxes, and they will sell the rest of the plantation, two thousand acres of land." He waited for the people to finish their chorus of amens, then continued. "If we who founded New Canaan could buy this land, then we will have a real town—not just a settlement. All of you who is sharecropping have a chance to buy your own land too. If you form a land association and everyone pay monthly dues, then the association will buy the land and divide it equally among the members." People murmured in agreement.

When the meeting was over, the people from the Phillips plantation rushed up to Obi, anxious to hear his narrative to add to the growing number of stories about the old plantation, the war, the Yankees, the time of freedom. He met Virginia and George and their sons, Melissa, Brother Paul, Isabel. He remembered them all. Then Rose introduced him to the teacher, Miss Fortune. "Easter is staying with Miss Fortune's family," Rose informed him. He took an instant liking to Miss Fortune, since her family was caring for his Easter.

As they walked home, the air was pungent with the scent of salt water and pine and noisy with the sounds of crickets and croaking frogs. The stars seemed close and bright, and Obi felt as though he could pick one out of the sky and send it to Easter in the purse he had bought her.

"Obi, people happy to see you," Rose said. "Even the ones who don't know you."

"I'm happy to see them too."

He sat at Rose's table and wrote two letters that night.

First, he wrote to Major Delany's assistant to let him know what had happened to the children. He asked him to find out when the next army transport was coming through, and told him he'd send the children to Edisto Island if he couldn't find anyone to take them in.

He also wrote Easter, letting her know that he had arrived safely in New Canaan and that Rose made sure he saw all of the Phillips's people. He told her about the meeting.

When I listen to Julius and the others talk about land it make me think that we can have a sweet life here among the oaks and palmettoes. I save enough money to buy land, so I don't have to join no asssociation. And I been thinking too. I want to build my own carpenter business. The only farming I will do is to grow enough food to feed us. And I never want to work for another man again in my life.

I cannot wait for you to return, so that I can hold you in my arms once again. I am happy for the first time in my life.

Your Obi

8

Your door is shut against my tightened face,
And I am sharp as steel with discontent.
—CLAUDE McKAY

The next day Obi began to organize his life. Samuel took him to one of the frequent plantation auctions, where the owners were selling off everything from farm tools to furniture to pay taxes. Obi purchased a pair of overalls and carpentry tools: an adze, a chisel, and a handsaw. Since they were riding in Samuel's mule cart, Samuel also offered to show Obi the important places on the island.

"Now, you know where the church, the school, and Miss Mary's store is. That's the hub of the island. The black hub. I'm going to show you the other side of the island."

"What's on the other side?"

"The white hub," he explained. "Elenaville. Them wealthy planters use to keep summer mansions there. Since the war many of them living there year-round 'cause they lose their plantation. You get a lot of carpentry work at the 'capital,' " he chuckled. "That's what we call Elenaville. 'Cause the people them think they so capital." He threw his head back and laughed loudly at his own joke.

Obi smiled, enjoying the way Samuel found himself so amusing. As they rode along Obi reviewed the plans he'd made so far. That was one thing the army had taught him—the importance of planning and organization. He had insisted that when the cotton began to open in August, he would help Rose in her fields, to make up for bringing the children. She insisted, however, that he share in her profits from the cotton. Obi didn't want to waste time. In the two weeks before the cotton opened, he would begin to lay the foundation for his own carpentry business.

He'd use the money saved from his army pay to purchase more land, and the money he made from his carpentry and growing cotton with Rose would help him to buy the materials he needed in order to build his own home.

"Samuel, there be a newspaper on this island?"

"Yes. The office is in Elenaville. You want to buy a paper?"

"No, man. I'm advertising for my carpentry business."

Samuel glanced at Obi as though he were impressed. "That's a smart thing you doing."

When the forest began to thin out, Obi saw a cluster of houses in the distance. "That's it," Samuel said. "That's Elenaville."

Obi liked the way the village sat on a bluff overlooking the water; its homes spread out from the center of the small business area. Part of the narrow street had been turned into a marketplace crowded with black farmers selling eggs, shrimp, crab, catfish, peas, melons, figs, and chickens. Samuel waved and called out greetings to the people he knew. They rode past a dress shop, a general store, and a sweet shop. Obi spotted the newspaper office a few feet from an unused lodge where the planters used to socialize.

Obi jumped out of the mule cart. "I won't be long."

"Take your time. I going back down to the market and speak to some of my friends while you take care of your business." He started to turn the mule cart around.

Obi gazed at the homes that stretched to the end of the street and sat on the bluff beyond. "Think I'll call at some of them homes and see if they need a carpenter. Got my new tools and could start working today perhaps."

"Meet me at the market when you done."

Obi walked inside the office and approached a man sitting behind a desk. "I want to put an ad in your paper," Obi shouted over the clatter of the printing press in the next room.

"All right. What you want to say? You looking for a family member? Tell me slowly and carefully so's I can understand, and I'll write it for you."

The man dipped his pen in the inkwell and took a piece of paper from a stack sitting on his desk. "That'll be one dollar to keep your ad in for a week and fifty cents for writing it out for you. You understand?"

Obi balled his hand into a fist to keep himself from snatching the paper away from him. Evidentally a lot of black people had been putting ads in the paper, looking for missing relatives. And most of them could neither read nor write.

"I can write it myself."

"You know how to write?"

Obi's temple began to throb. "I said I will write it out myself."

"You got to write clear and correct."

Obi wrote quickly and legibly as the man watched in amazement.

Position wanted: Master Carpenter can do any kind of building and repair work. Contact, Mr. O. Booker, General Store, New Canaan.

"Are you Mr. Booker?" the man asked.

"Naw sir, that's my massa. He the one show me how to write this."

The man looked perplexed, as if he didn't know whether or not to believe him.

Obi reached in his pocket and removed his billfolder. "Keep it in for five weeks," he said impatiently, throwing five dollars on the desk and rushing out of the office before he was asked another stupid question.

He walked toward the end of the street, where the church and parsonage stood and the homes began. He was surprised to see on close inspection that the first house he approached wasn't as sturdy and well kept as it appeared from a distance. He tried not to feel like a beggar as he walked around to the back of the small one-story home, where he noticed that some of the shutters were missing and that the roof badly needed repair.

He breathed deeply, fighting his shyness, and knocked on the door. The young woman who answered appeared to be as ramshackle as her home. Maybe she too was once elegant. "I need a lot of work around here. I can give you food and a place to stay." She pointed to a shed off to the side of her house. "We can't afford to pay you wages."

"Thank you, ma'am," Obi said and quickly walked away. He already had food and a shed to sleep in. At the next house he opened the rickety gate and walked around to the back. An old man with thick white hair accused him of being a beggar and a vagrant and threatened to call the sheriff. Obi started to give up. But he reminded himself why he was going from door to door. *Can't let a fool stop me.*

Another man offered him a sharecropping arrangement. "Don't have to pay rent for the cabin, and you get half the crop."

He refused, knowing that most sharecroppers were left at the end of the season with only a pile of debt after purchasing overpriced supplies from the planters who hired them. Obi went to each home in the town, and every time either he was turned away or no one was around. Every home he saw needed some kind of repair. None were as strong and sturdy as they appeared from a distance.

He took another deep breath and walked briskly to the last home in the cluster of houses near the center of town. This one was in the best shape of all of them. Two long porches ran the entire width of the stately two-story house. The house had an unobstructed view of the water, and he imagined how the golden-red sunsets must look from the second-story porch. Obi stepped into the yard and continued to admire the home.

A dog barked, and a tall, heavy-set middle-aged man opened the door. "Yes?"

Obi remained standing at the bottom of the steps. "I'm a carpenter, sir, and I'm looking to see if you need any work done."

"No. I don't need a carpenter. I need men to work on my plantation, Fair Oaks."

"I don't do field work, sir. I'm a carpenter."

"I'm paying six dollars a month. If you live in one of my cabins, then it be five dollars a month."

"Thank you, sir," Obi said and calmly started to walk away.

"Wait," the man called him back. "You're wasting your time. The cotton is opening, and planters need field hands. Anyway, you need a special license to be a carpenter. You have that?"

"That law's been struck down," Obi said. "New state constitution says no more special licenses." *Didn't need a license when I was a slave.*

The man glared at him. "You a Republican, huh? You people better wake up. Them Yankees don't mean you no good."

"I'm a master carpenter." Obi's temples began to throb as he tried to remain calm.

The man laughed. "Master carpenter, huh? I need a good field hand, and you look like a big, strong boy to me."

Before Obi thought about what he was doing, he bounded up the steps, snatched the man by the collar, and nearly lifted him off the ground. "I'm not a boy. I'm a man. A master carpenter."

The man turned a deep shade of pink, and Obi put him down. He rushed out of the yard as the man ran back into the house. Obi wouldn't run like a criminal, but he walked quickly back into the center of town, where he saw Samuel, sitting on a crate and talking to one of the farmers. "Hey, Sam. We better go," Obi said, looking nervously toward the cluster of houses.

"What's wrong with you?"

"Tell you later. It's best we go now." Obi's tone was sharp and edgy. He turned to the farmer. "If a white man come here asking about me, tell him you ain't see me."

Samuel looked puzzled. "Obi, what—?"

Obi practically lifted Samuel into the mule cart. "Come on! I tell you on the way. Hurry, man."

The mule cart rattled as they rode into the forest, and Obi continued glancing backward as Samuel shouted nervously, "Obi, would you please tell me what I running from, so I can be as upset as you is?"

Obi, still glancing backward, told Samuel what had happened.

Samuel slowed the mule cart. "You did what?"

"Why you slowing down?"

"Ain't nobody chasing us, and nobody will be chasing us," Samuel said, throwing his head back and laughing loudly. He made almost as much noise as the flock of cawing crows overhead. "It not that funny. That's how trouble start, over one small incident." Obi's eyes appeared heavy and weary as he told Samuel about what had happened to Grace and her family in Pine Bluff, Arkansas. "Could be there was some little argument between a white and a black and the black man sass the white man and the whole black settlement was attacked and people killed, man. Same thing happen in Memphis and New Orleans. A little incident turn into a riot, and a lot of blacks killed by white mobs."

"That never happen here. Too many of us on this island. The only whites is the few you see in Elenaville. They 'fraid to come into our village. Yankees be the only whites who come deep into where we live." Samuel slowed the mules to a leisurely pace, his round face smiling easily.

"Now, this is not to say that the man wouldn't put some buckshot in your hind parts if he'd had a chance to get hold of his shotgun."

Obi relaxed his body. "Just didn't want to bring no trouble to New Canaan. You know I placed the ad in the paper."

"Just hope he's not the one who answers your ad," Samuel chuckled. "Every time I think on it, Obi, I get tickled. Wish I could've seen you snatch that man up in his collar. "

"Now wouldn't that be something, if he answers the ad," Obi said.

"Well, he say he didn't want a carpenter, so he wouldn't be answering ads. Anyway, Obi, the only work most people get 'round here is sharecropping, except for those of us who own our land."

Obi listened to the call of the seabirds—a comforting sound, reminding him of his first letter from Easter. "Samuel," he said, "I will never sharecrop or sign a work contract. No man will ever have a piece of paper on me saying they own my labor. I'm helping Rose bring in her crop, but that's different. Rose is a friend."

"Well, Obi, you'll need to buy land, grow your own cotton, and make your money that way. This carpenter business you talking about, I don't know. Seem like we can't get that kind of work no more. The only work we get is field hand or sharecropping. I thank God every day for making it so that I have my own land."

"People tell me I wouldn't be able to find Easter, but I was determined and I find her. Now, I'm determined to have my own carpentry business." He gazed at Rose's property in the distance. The setting sun spread a bronze glow over the chicken coop, the well, and the animal pen.

"Sam, if I fall into the farming and sharecropping, I'll lose what I'm really after. I mean to be truly free."

"Sometime, Obi, you have no choice. You have to eat. Take care of your family."

"That be true, but I have the choice not to sign a work contract. I will farm only to grow food for my own table."

"Sometime we have to do things we don't want to do," Samuel said.

"But it don't have to be sharecropping. And I don't have to sign a contract. No man will ever rule over me again."

"Tomorrow be another day, Obi. Someone might answer your ad."

9

*The third morning it was the same work over again. There were
forty children present, many of them large boys and girls.
I had already a list of over forty names.*

—ELIZABETH HYDE BOTUME, TEACHER, FREEDMEN'S SCHOOL

August 1868

"Rosie, how did you and Simon manage to plant six acres of cotton by
yourselves?" Obi asked as he inspected the leaves of an unopened
cotton plant.

She stopped working for a moment and wiped her forehead with
the back of her hand. "Virginia and George help me. Now they sharecropping for Julius." She shielded her eyes from the sun. "This sun
sap all your strength," she sighed. They resumed walking down the
rows of cotton plants. "It was a godsend when you show up. I didn't
know how me and Simon was going to do all of this work alone."
Rose moved on, deftly pulling the cotton bolls out of their pods and
dropping them into her sack.

Obi continued also. He had begun to fall into the rhythm and life
of the village, except he didn't go to the praise house on Thursdays or
to church on Sundays. It wasn't his habit. He'd lived a solitary life on
the Jennings farm, close only to Easter, Jason, and the old African,
Buka. When Easter and Jason went to religious services with the Phil-

lips's slaves, Obi and Buka spent Sundays fishing. This Sunday he planned to begin digging the foundation for his and Easter's new home.

He carefully checked the leaves of the unopened cotton plants, making sure that they were not too dark and that none of the unopened pods had dropped to the ground, a sign of the dreaded blight. But the leaves looked green and healthy.

He stopped for a moment, wiping the sweat out of his eyes, and he spotted a female figure in the distance at the edge of the field. As she drew nearer he realized that it was Miss Fortune, the teacher.

"Mr. Booker, excuse me for troubling you."

"No bother, miss."

"I know that the children of farm families must work until the winter, but some youngsters begin school in September. Others in January. Were you planning to send your children, I mean the children you're caring for, to school?"

She sound exactly like a northern Yankee. "I don't know how long they'll be with us."

"Miss Rose has told me how you came to have them. They are probably better off with you and Miss Rose caring for them." Her voice was soft and light, and Obi had to strain to understand her. "The work farms or camps can be hard on children who have no relatives to protect them. I'm making inquiries through the missionary society as to whether a family would take them in. But in the meantime they can come to our school."

"Yes, they ought to go to school," he said in an unsure voice. "The boy can go while he's here. The girl has trouble seeing, she says. I don't think there's much she can learn."

"There's an excellent school for the blind in Boston. I'll make inquiries about all of that. We charge a small fee, only to those families who can afford it. Would a dollar fifty a month be too much?"

"No. I guess that be fine."

"I see the little boy helps Miss Mary in her store."

Obi smiled. "Yes, she took a liking to him. He makes ten cents a week and is proud of it."

"He's a charming bright-eyed little fellow." She held out her hand, and Obi, embarrassed, wiped his hand on his overalls before taking hers.

"Thank you for your time, Mr. Booker. School will open the end of September."

When Obi, Rose, and Simon left the fields just before dusk, they saw Scipio racing toward them, waving an envelope. He delivered the mail to nearby neighbors for Miss Mary. "It's for you, Mr. Obi."

"It probably from Easter." Rose's eyes sparkled.

Obi tried to speak calmly, but his heart was racing. "Come on, we read Easter's letter when we get home."

When they reached the cabin, Rose sat expectantly, almost child-like, across from him at the table. "Hurry up and read it, Obi," she urged.

August 5, 1868

Dear Obi,

I couldn't wait to give you and Rose this good news. I have been offered wages to work as an assistant teacher. Can you imagine that? Me? Easter? Who not long ago didn't even have a last name. I will work at the orphanage, with the principal teacher. The orphanage is so overcrowded that they need extra workers. Not only will I teach, I will also assist the Director in making sure that the older children who are bound out to families are being treated properly.

This means that I will not be able to come home by September as I had thought, but will be back home in May. This opportunity will help me to be an even better teacher when I return to New Canaan. I could open my own school one day, and I will be earning my own keep for the first time in my life. I will earn twenty dollars a month, and will no longer be a charity girl, but will be able to pay the Fortunes for my room and board. I will have money for what we need for our new home and new life, as well.

Obi, I long to see you. You, Rose, and Jason are my whole life. But staying a while longer gives you time to build a home for us as well as time for you to settle into New Canaan. I wanted to try and come home for a visit at Christmas, but that is the busiest time. I was told that many parents leave their children in the orphanage just so that the youngsters will have some warmth and food for the holidays.

Miss Fortune wrote me and told me that she met you. She also told me about some children you and Rose are helping. So we are both in the business of helping children. What are their names?

I have thought long and hard about this, but Obi, if you do not want me to stay longer, I will come home as planned in September and train under Miss Fortune; however, as I told you, teachers who work for the Society cannot be married. So, we'd still have to wait.

Obi, thank you for the beautiful purse. It is my most treasured possession, besides you. (laugh) Give everyone my love. Especially, Rose.

Love, Easter

Obi felt as though a hand with long, icy fingers had squeezed out the little bit of joy that had begun to enter his heart. He was speechless. Confused.

"After all of this time waiting, she's not coming back?"

"She didn't say she wasn't coming back. She have a chance to teach and continue to learn, is what she say."

"She can teach and learn right here." Obi's eyes looked fiery one moment and pained the next. "I'm telling her to come back here and work with Miss Fortune. At least I can be near her."

"If you tell her to return, she will. Obi, see how ignorant most of us is? Can't read. Can't write. Don't know nothing except what white folk tell us.

"Look at you, Obi. Suppose you never run away. Suppose you just wait for someone to tell you that you free instead of taking your own freedom. You'd be just as ignorant of things of the world as you was when you was a slave."

"I've waited so long."

"Least you know where she is. Easter always been smart. Always want more'n what people say she should have. Easter could work with Miss Fortune, but even someone as ignorant as me know that she learn more working in Philadelphia. Look at what Easter could show us. I mean people like me and the children who she'll teach. When she come back here she bring a big world with her."

Suddenly he felt empty and tired. Maybe Thomas was right. Maybe he should have just gone out West with him and Peter.

"She'll come back," Rose continued. "We all she have." Her dark eyes pleaded with him to understand. "She have no people up North. And Easter wouldn't leave the people she love." She paused to listen to her own words—to make sure that they rang true in her own ears.

He answered Easter's letter later that evening in the privacy of the shed. By the light of a candle, with Rose's words ringing in his ears, he wrote:

August 20, 1868

Dear Easter,

I hope that you are feeling fine. I am sorry that you will not be back here when you said. I try to understand why you want to stay, but I do not understand how we can be separated for eight years and you are not coming home when you plan to. Next spring seem a long time, and I want us to begin our life together now. Easter, you always have your own mind, so I will not try to tell you what to do. Complete your studies, but I will come to Philadelphia to visit you for Christmas. That way I can finish helping Rose bring in her cotton crop. We can marry in Philadelphia and not wait forever to start our new life together. I want us to be husband and wife.

Easter, you do not have to worry about working. I will take care of you.

Love, Obi

P.S. The names of the children Rose and I care for are Grace, Scipio and Araba. By the way, have you heard from Jason?

He lay across his pallet and closed his eyes. He hoped that Rose was right. That Easter would return.

10

*From a very dark cloud in the sky the most vivid flashes of
lightning were continually breaking. There seemed not
a second's pause between the flashes.*
—*CHARLOTTE FORTEN*, THE JOURNALS OF
CHARLOTTE FORTEN GRIMKE

September 1868

Every Friday evening Obi faithfully attended the meeting of the New
Canaan Republican Club, going straight from the fields where he was
helping Rose to the meeting in the church. He wanted to know when
land became available, and he was interested in what was happening in
politics and the government. He especially wanted to know about his
rights and privileges as a freedman and a veteran.

As he neared the church, he saw men and a few women milling
around outside. He stopped by Miss Mary's store first to see whether
he had any mail. He expected to get a letter from Easter soon, and
hoped there'd be one from the bureau or Miss Jeffries. Or maybe
there'd be a letter in response to his carpenter's ad.

He liked the store's scent of teas and spices. "Evening, Mr.
Booker," Miss Mary said. "I think something came for you this evening. The ferry was late today, and I already sent Scipio home."

Obi rifled through the large basket on the counter that contained the mail while Miss Mary chattered on. He had a letter from Easter, and another letter bearing the seal of the Freedmen's Bureau in Beaufort.

"Thank you, Miss Mary," he said, and bought a two-cent bag of gumdrops for the children.

He rushed out of the store, but before he went into the meeting, he leaned against one of the oak trees and tried to read the letters in the gathering dusk and the thick purple clouds rolling in from the sea. He read the letter from the major's assistant first. The assistant advised Obi that there would be no military transport going to Edisto Island until the end of December. However, if he were able to take the children there himself to the government work farm, the bureau would remit to him any expenses he incurred.

Obi decided to wait for the transport in December. He had no time to take them, and there was always the possibility that a home could be found for them on Santa Elena Island. He excitedly tore open the letter from Easter.

September 3, 1868

Dear Obi,

I hope all is well with you, Rose and the children you are caring for and all of my friends in New Canaan. I am quite fine. Obi, I fear that you are angry and do not understand why I want to extend my stay here. I am not only learning about teaching, but I am also learning, as my instructor tells me, how to help the needy and how to run an institution.

When I look on the faces of these frightened orphan children, I see us, Obi. And when I see how a few softly spoken, comforting words can brighten their faces, then I feel that this is the work I must be doing. I am learning so much and will be able to be a good teacher when I return. My instructor says that I could be a headmis-

tress in a school for girls. Obi, I have not abandoned you or Jason and I do want us to be husband and wife and have a real family. But I also want to be able to teach and to learn as much as I can.

Obi, if I teach for the society, even there in Santa Elena, I cannot be a married woman or have children of my own. But the same rules do not apply if I run my own school, and this is why I need the special training. Certainly Santa Elena Island needs many schools. One of these days the missionaries will leave. There is growing antagonism here in the North against the freedmen. People say that now that the war is over and slavery has ended, it is time to think about other things. They are saying that there is no need for the soldiers to be there and for the Freedmen's Bureau to be there. They are sick and tired of the war and of the problems of the freed people. One day the missionaries will leave and the schools will close unless we, the freed people, are able at last to stand up for ourselves and teach our own.

Obi, I love you. Freedom would be bitter without you. You, Jason, Rose are the only kin I have. New Canaan is the only real home I have. I am not doing this because I don't want us to have a life together, I am doing this so that we can have a good life together.

If you come to Philadelphia and we marry here, then I cannot continue with my work. I do not want us to live up here. Instead of spending money to come here to be with me, even though I want you to very much, I think you shouldn't use up money in that way. I want to come back to our home, and I want to marry in New Canaan with all my "chosen" family near me. My heart is in New Canaan.

With love, Easter

P.S. I received a letter from Jason last week. He is in Ohio in a big tent show! He tells me that he sings, dances and plays the banjo. He is no longer with Doctor Taylor.

He kissed her letter and then put it in his pocket, next to his bill-folder. He'd read it again later, so that he could fix the sound of her voice and her reassuring words in his head. Obi suddenly realized that the voice he heard now was no longer that of the young girl he'd left behind. She had grown into a woman. A good woman. He missed her nonetheless. Though the eight months until she returned stretched before him like an eternity, his spirit was lifted as he walked toward the church.

As soon as he entered the building, Obi knew that there was an important visitor because the meeting was more crowded than usual. He spotted several men from New Canaan sitting in the front, proudly looking up at Julius, as they did at every meeting. Obi sat in the back, as usual, next to Samuel.

Julius said only a few words about the new constitution and the elections in November, when he, along with a number of other black men, would be running for office. Julius was running for a seat on the new South Carolina legislature. He also told them about the mounting violence against the freedmen.

"We safe down here in these island because there is more of us than them Ku Kluxers, but we have to be vigilant. These are dangerous times, especially when you in politics."

Samuel poked Obi in his ribs. "Can you imagine that? He been in slavery, and now he going to be a lawmaker?"

Obi agreed. Julius had prospered. He also knew many Yankees who were buying land and the old plantation houses on the island. He'd talk to him after the meeting and find out whether he knew anyone who needed a carpenter.

Julius proudly introduced his visitor, a distinguished-looking black man with a full beard. Julius bowed to him and the audience. "Brothers, this is Senator Benjamin Randolph, from Orangeburg. As some of you know, Senator Randolph was a chaplain in the Twenty-sixth Colored Infantry. He is a teacher, a newspaper owner, a county school commissioner, and the chairman of the Republican State Committee.

Yes, sir. We are proud to have you with us, Senator." Julius didn't talk long when visitors came. He was embarrassed about his own humble beginnings when in the company of better-educated black men who were freeborn.

Randolph talked about the upcoming elections and the importance of voting the Republican ticket. "The Democrats are trying to lure the freedmen away from the Republican party. Do not be tricked by their lies."

Samuel poked Obi in the ribs again. "He right about that. A black man ain't got no business joining them Democrats. Every rebel is a Democrat."

When the meeting ended, people gathered around Julius and the senator. Samuel turned to Obi. "Come on, let's shake this important man's hands."

Obi followed him. "I just want to ask Julius something. That man probably tired and don't want all of them people crowding around him, shaking his hands."

"Well, he's gonna shake my hand if he want my vote."

Obi stood outside the group of people and waited patiently until he caught Julius's eye. "Julius, can I speak with you a moment?"

Obi saw Julius's annoyed glance, which he quickly tried to hide.

"Yes, yes," Julius said impatiently. "But you'll have to wait." He turned and smiled as he shook hands with a very tall, slender white man.

Obi had to walk away or he would have snatched Julius up in his collar and reminded him of where he came from. He wondered what he'd done to offend Julius. Had they ever had an argument when they were boys? He couldn't remember any incidents. Obi left the church and waited for Samuel, who came outside shortly after.

"Obi, I heard how Julius answer you. I guess he a big man now. I'm surprised at him, though. We his people, and he always make time for us."

"It's not important," Obi said.

As they walked away from the church, darkness covered them like a great black cloak. The still air was heavy with moisture and silence. "Might get some rain tonight," Samuel mused. A little smile played around his mouth. "By the way, I notice you been framing out a house on Easter's property."

"Yes."

"So you and her is getting married? That's what I been hearing."

"Where you been hearing this from?" Obi knew the answer before Samuel told him. Rose.

"Rose tell my wife, and she tell a next person. That's the way of these villagers, Obi. And if they don't know your story, they make one up for you."

"Yes, me and Easter getting married." He'd have to tell Rose not to talk his business. Suddenly Obi understood Julius's attitude. Everyone in the village knew that he and Easter were going to marry. Maybe Julius was sweet on Easter. Obi smiled to himself. Imagine that. He'd ask Rose about it. She would know. Samuel broke into his thoughts.

"Obi, you a fine carpenter. The wood so perfect. You buy it?"

"I buy the logs, then I finish them off myself."

"If you need help anytime, ask me. It cost a lot of money to buy them logs."

"I'm just taking my time." Obi didn't want to insult Samuel, but he had no faith in the carpentry skills of the men in the village. He wanted more than the kind of rough cabins they built. He'd used more of his savings than he had intended, but he wanted a lovely home—like the one he admired in Elenaville.

"Well, anytime you need help, I'm here. That's how we do, you know. The people help each other put up their homes."

"I'm just taking my time with it," Obi repeated.

When the shelled road ended, they heard rumbling in the distance.

"Well, good night to you, Obi," Samuel said. "Sounds like God's going to water them fields for us."

Obi turned into the path leading to Rose's cabin. When he saw the soft glow of candlelight under her doorsill, he knew that she was still awake. Claps of thunder were more frequent, and he felt a few drops of rain just before entering the cabin. The boys were asleep on their pallets. Simon's loud snoring filled the cabin, almost drowning out the thunder. Little Ray wouldn't sleep in the room with his mother and the girls anymore, but insisted on staying with Simon and Scipio.

Rose slept soundly too, sitting on her rocking chair. Her head dangled to the side, and the patchwork quilt she was making had fallen at her feet. Obi gently shook her by the shoulders. "Rosie, you going to get a crick in your neck."

"Obi, I was waiting for you. How was the meeting?" She picked up the quilt and continued stitching. He gave her the news and then told her about the letter from the bureau.

"You know, I grow use to those children. And the girl been a help to me, but she need some kind of schooling."

"A school for the blind," Obi said.

"She not really blind. How can she be? She been helping make this quilt. The girl just don't like to go outside."

"If she go to the work farm talking about only seeing inside the house and going blind when she outside, they put her in the insane asylum," Obi mused. "I'll wait till December before I send them to the farm. Scipio have a chance for a little schooling here."

"That's all he talk about. Going to school," Rose said. "Miss Mary say she'd take in Scipio and raise him, but I told her he shouldn't be separated from his sisters. I been asking around though. It's just hard to get someone to take in all three."

He gazed at Scipio, sleeping contentedly, far removed from the frightened, ragged child he'd found a few months ago. "I hope we can find someone here to take them in soon. But it have to be the right someone," Obi said.

A loud clap of thunder startled them both. Suddenly, it sounded as though the sky had opened and that the cabin had plunged into the middle of a waterfall.

"We need this rain," Rose said as she stood up and lay the quilt across the rocker. "Thought we was fixing to have a dry drought." She walked over to the fireplace. "Kept the okra soup warm for you."

His mouth watered as she dished out the soup for him. "Rose"—he smiled slightly—"Julius sweet on Easter?"

She nearly dropped the bowl. "Where you hear that story?"

"Just a thought I had."

She handed him the bowl and sat down. Her large, expressive eyes slid around her face as she avoided his stare. "Come on, Rosie. You ain't going to lie to me, are you?"

"Yes. I suppose he was. But she ain't sweet on him. I know that. She only think of one man in this world. You. Who tell you?"

"Nobody. I know by the way Julius act toward me. Unfriendly. Like I did him something. Just wanted to ask whether he knew anyone who needed a carpenter."

Her eyes sparkled in a teasing way. "Obi, you ain't the friendliest person. Some of the people 'round here think you don't like them. And you don't go to church like everybody else."

"Don't tell me about church no more, Rose. God be everywhere."

She sucked her teeth. "You like to be alone too much, Obi. Anyway, Easter love you. You don't have no worry with that."

Suddenly, thunder exploded around them. Little Ray woke up, crying, and Rose picked him up. Scipio sat up with a start, his eyes wide and terrified. And then they heard a roar so loud and deep it sounded and felt as though a train had run under the house. Grace screamed and ran out of the bedroom, holding Araba. Even Simon woke up with a big question mark on his face.

Obi opened the shutter slightly and peeped out of the window. The trees swayed like a circle of dancers. "This a bad one," he said, quickly closing the shutter. He walked toward the door. "I'm taking my tools and my haversack out of the shed, before it fall down."

"I don't think you should go out there now." She patted little Ray on his back as he buried his face in her neck.

"Easter's letters and my army papers are in the sack."

"Obi, that shed stand up to many a storm."

He slowly opened the door. "I ain't taking no chances."

"You taking a big chance going out there. You have Easter's address in your memory, don't you? And you can buy more tools. Can't replace yourself."

Obi turned to Scipio and then Grace. "You all go on back to sleep. Nothing to be scared of." Then he said to Rose, "It's just a few steps to the shed." He paused a moment with his hand on the door latch. "Hope this wind skip over my house I ain't even finish yet."

"You better hope it skip over you," Rose warned.

As soon as he stepped outside, the raging wind knocked him against the cabin. He went back inside and handed Rose his billfolder. "Don't want to lose this. The wind is raising Cain out there."

He went outside again, thrusting his head and his shoulders forward like a bull charging the wind. He thought that he heard Rose calling him as he fought his way to the shed. The wind lashed him like a cruel master. Falling to the ground, he attempted to crawl to the shed and was thrown into a tree trunk. He saw nothing. Obi continued to crawl in what he thought was the direction of the shed. He attempted to stand up in the midst of a deafening roar and a thunderous crash. A heavy object hit the side of his head, knocking him back down. The pain was so sharp, he felt as if his insides were rising from his stomach, filling his mouth.

He crawled through the mud, still determined to reach the shed. Lightning crackled and flashed as bright as daylight. He saw the chicken coop, the animal pen, and the shed. In an instant, a massive dark form crashed to the ground, obliterating everything under it. The shed, the animal pen, and the chicken coop were gone.

Through sheer will, he pulled his prone body up and stumbled and staggered away from the shed, back toward Rose's cabin. Another round of steady lightning illuminated his way, but he didn't see the cabin. It was gone. The wind knocked him into a bush that tore at his flesh. He thought that he heard the children crying. He thought that he saw the cabin again. *A dream and then I die.*

11

I've been in the storm so long
You know I've been in the storm so long,
Oh Lord, give me more time to pray,
I've been in the storm so long.

—AFRICAN AMERICAN SPIRITUAL

Obi felt as though someone were banging loudly on his head with a mallet and every bone in his body had been snapped in two. Something dripped on his hands and arms. *Hell must be wet.* He thought he heard a voice calling him and slowly opened his eyes. Grace peered down at him. A beautiful image. He wasn't dead. He looked up at the ceiling. Part of it was badly damaged, and he could see a patch of blue sky. The water was coming from the roof.

"Mr. Obi? You awake?"

He groaned.

Rose, her face tight and pinched, bent over him also. "Told you not to go out there, Obi. Almost get yourself killed."

He slowly pushed himself up and wondered how he'd ended up on a pallet in front of the fireplace and why the banging in his head wouldn't stop. He turned toward the window and saw Simon banging a peg into one of the shutters with a stick. "Rosie," he croaked, "tell him to stop. I'll fix the shutter."

"You ain't in no condition to fix anything." She straightened up and ordered Grace to make Obi a cup of tea and Simon to sweep the water out of the cabin.

"You all okay? I thought the cabin was gone," Obi said.

"We thought you was gone. The children was crying and I was peeping out of the window the whole time you were out there. The lightning help me see when you stumble and fall. Me and Simon drag you back in here."

"Where the children?" he asked, rubbing his aching head.

"In the other room. Sleep. They was scared and crying most of the night. But they settle down when morning come and the storm pass. You was soundly knocked out, Obi. Slept through the rest of the storm."

Obi struggled to his feet. Rose whispered so softly that he could barely hear her. "Even Grace cry. I never see her cry before," she said.

"She's scared." He rubbed his sore legs.

"She scared that you die out there. You all she have."

Obi hobbled to the table, wondering why Rose was talking foolishness at a time like this. He called to Simon as Grace handed him a cup of tea. "When I finish this tea, we go get them tools out of the shed and fix—" He stopped himself and gulped down his tea. "Rose, you looked outside yet?"

"No, didn't have time to." She shook her head sadly. "Maybe I was afraid of what I see." She rubbed her head. "My God, Obi. If that cotton be ruined, then I lose everything."

Obi stood up stiffly. "I'm going to see." He hoped that he'd only imagined a massive object falling on the shed, just as he'd imagined that the cabin had been destroyed. His memory was foggy.

"Maybe you should rest a while longer," Rose broke into his thoughts. "Simon can get water if we still have the tin tub, and you can go in the other room and clean that mud off of you." Her movements were nervous, as though she wanted to find things to do in the cabin. As long as she didn't see, she didn't know.

Obi understood. "I'll go. You stay here."

She wiped her hands nervously on her apron. "I'll go with you." She put her shawl around her shoulders.

The door barely hung on its hinges. "Rosie, me and Simon fix the window and door easily," Obi said, trying to sound hopeful for her. "But the first thing is the roof." He walked to the door and opened it very carefully so that it didn't fall on them.

He and Rose were speechless as they looked outside. It was as if the cabin had been lifted up and dropped off in a different place. Rose's kitchen garden and clean, well-swept yard were covered with a thick layer of mud. The azalea bushes, strewn over the yard, had become scraggly piles of sticks with dead leaves hanging off them. The shed, the chicken coop, the animal pen, all had disappeared under the oak tree. Obi guessed that the mule and the cow had been crushed under the oak too, along with his tools, his letters from Easter, and a few meager belongings.

Past Rose's yard, he could see clear over to the shelled road. Where cabins used to stand in the distance, he saw emptiness.

"Thank God you wasn't in that shed," Rose muttered.

They trudged through thick mud and skirted around downed trees. When they reached her fields they found complete devastation— cotton, potatoes, and corn, all gone. "At least we alive. My home still standing, and the land still here." Rose smiled as tears rolled down her cheeks. "There's nothing to do but start again."

"Start with what?"

She held out her hands, her fingers long and strong. "Start with these." She tapped her forehead. "And this. God give me these two things. He save my son." She stared at Obi. "He save my friends. God is good. God will provide," she said, her hands slightly trembling, her lips speaking words of hope, her eyes sorrowful as she gazed at a year's worth of work, turned to mud. "Come, let's see how you and Easter's property look."

"I know ain't nothing standing. I don't need to see just now." He didn't want to face his loss at that moment. He'd seen enough devastation.

She insisted. "Sometime a storm touch one field and skip over another."

They trudged to where they thought Easter's property began. "Obi, I ain't too sure. I wouldn't be able to tell where Easter's land is if my cabin wasn't still standing."

Rose's cabin was like a compass pointing in the direction of Easter's property, which had no more landmarks. The pine trees, the bushes, the fig trees, all gone as though they had been picked up and tossed away by an angry god to another muddy field. Then he saw one of the beams he'd meticulously crafted, split and broken and almost completely covered with mud. The foundation he so carefully made with oyster shells and sand, destroyed. He felt as empty inside as the stripped fields around him. The home he'd started building now a gaping, muddy pit. A home wiped away before it was even built.

Rose's voice sounded so far away; Obi felt as though he were distant, removed. "Obi, you start again, is all. This not the end of everything."

It was the end of everything as far as he could tell.

They stood in the field like lost, helpless children. Rose spoke first. "We don't know why things happen, but there must be a reason," she said. "We are not to question." Her shoulders sagged. "Last year it was the blight, and I did everything the way Rayford teach me. I manage to make twenty-five dollars from the cotton, enough to pay the taxes on this land. And we had enough food for us and the animals."

"You ain't no farmer. It was different when Rayford was here with you. You a cook." He tried to say something to make her feel better.

"Your food was the best thing about working on the Phillips plantation when Jennings send me and Easter over there."

"What I should do then, cook in the middle of the field and sell the food?"

"You should rest them cotton field and just grow what you going to eat."

"Cotton is the only thing bring in money. There be taxes due."

Then anger rose up in him. "A cotton field is a curse." He spit on the ground. "It ain't never bring us the money it used to bring them slave owners." His head throbbed. "See, when them planters have a lot of land and slaves, they sell off a slave here and there if they have a bad crop. That way they get their money back. That's what we need—some slaves to sell," he said bitterly. "Rosie, that's why me and my ma got separated. Whoever own us had to sell us. Got more money for selling us separately." He picked up the broken beam and then threw it angrily back on the ground.

"This a time when we should pray."

He looked up at the murky sky. "I too angry to pray."

"You flying in the face of God. You can't question His wisdom."

"Rose, I'm not questioning God, I'm questioning why you keep working cotton. Maybe you could rent or sell some of your land and—"

She wouldn't let him finish. "I not selling none of this land. I give Easter the two acres because she help me, and we like kin anyway. Rayford already pay the highest price for this land. No, Obi, I cannot." And she broke down. Strong, sturdy Rose. And Obi's heart was filled with hatred for the island. It was like quicksand and would eventually pull you down into its suffocating, muddy depths.

He put his arm around her. "Come, now, Rose. We have to see about them children. I'll try and patch the roof before the whole thing cave in." Obi's legs and arms still ached as he limped away from the fields. For the remainder of the day he and Simon patched the roof and tried to strengthen the shutters so that they would last until he made new ones. Eventually Rose would need a new door and new floors as well.

Obi worked in pain, but the cabin was the only shelter they had, and it looked as though it was about to fall apart. Grace and Scipio helped Rose clean the yard and searched through the wreckage of trees and bushes for Obi's tools and haversack. Just before dusk, when the cries of the seabirds could be heard in the distance, Scipio shouted, "Mr. Obi, look what I found." Grinning proudly, he held up Obi's army uniform—filthy and torn.

"Throw that thing away!" he snapped and was immediately sorry when he saw the hurt look in Scipio's eyes. Before he could say anything else, Samuel and a few of the other men of the village hurried into the yard.

"We just checking on everyone, Obi," Samuel said, out of breath, his round face sweating even though it was cool. "People is suffering too bad. Miss Mary cabin fall down."

"She hurt?"

"No, she was in the store. But the schoolhouse is gone. The whole village be suffering."

A week after the storm, Obi wrote Easter:

September 25, 1868

Dear Easter,

We've had a terrible storm here, but do not worry. We are all safe and sound, except Rose has lost all of her crops. Fortunately, her cabin still stands, but in bad condition.

Our home that I'd started building is ruined. I should've just thrown together a log house that hugged the ground. I use half the money I saved to build us a home. Now the money and the home is gone.

Many people have lost everything, and death has called at almost every door. Your poor friend Miss Fortune lost the school and everything in it.

There is no farming on the island. Only cleaning up after the storm. People are leaving every day joining labor gangs and going to Georgia and Florida. There is nothing here. More people will lose their land now because they lost their crops and do not have money to pay their taxes. I have offered to give Rose the money for her taxes. She refused, unless I said it was a loan. So I will give her the money and call it a loan. But I will not take any money back from her.

The plans I made are ruined for now, but I will still come and see you for Christmas. By that time you should have heard from Jason. When I finish seeing you, then I will get Jason.

Easter, there is no chance for a decent life down here. I have three hundred dollars left from the money I saved—enough to buy land and enough to build a business. But not here. This island is like quicksand. It sucks you in and smothers you to death. I am afraid if I try to build again in New Canaan, I will lose everything. I will never sharecrop or sign a work contract.

For now, it is easier to help others than to start to build another house that gets blown away before I'm done. I will build a school cabin for Miss Fortune. I have also been helping some of the men in the village rebuild their homes. So, I am doing a lot of carpentry, but of course, this is merely to help people. There is no pay. I suspect that I could get carpentry work in Elenaville after this storm. I have put another ad in the paper.

I love you Easter and miss you very much.

Your Obi

12

The colored Senator from South Carolina
was shot down a day or two ago.
—LETTERS AND DIARY OF LAURA M. TOWNE

October 1868

"I wish we could pay you, Mr. Booker," Miss Fortune said, clasping her hands in front of her as though she were praying. Her soft brown eyes gazed kindly on Obi, Simon, and two other teenage boys who were helping put the finishing touches on the schoolhouse cabin.

"Letting me use these tools is payment enough." Miss Fortune had insisted that Obi borrow the new saws, chisels, an adze, and axes belonging to the missionary society whenever he needed them. Obi handed an ax to Simon. "You boys cut down those two small pines so that I can show you how to make a bench."

"It's the least the society can do." She lowered her voice even though no one could hear them. "As a matter of fact, Mr. Booker, as far as I am concerned the tools belong to you. If it weren't for you, we wouldn't have a schoolhouse."

She stared for a moment at the small cabin. "You don't know what this means to us, Mr. Booker. We couldn't hold classes in the church. So many people need medical care that the doctor has been using the church as a hospital." She shook her head. "And you know, the school lost everything. We don't have a book or a piece of paper."

"I'm sorry, miss, I truly am."

"But we have our minds. The children can memorize their verses and learn by listening until the society sends more books." She smiled so sweetly, Obi thought about his friend Thomas and what a nice lady she would be for him—two colored Yankees together, he chuckled to himself.

"Mr. Booker, I don't think you realize what a great thing you've done for the children."

"Miss Fortune, we should be able to finish the benches by tomorrow and get some kindling for the stove, and you'll be ready for school. And we'll patch up your cabin."

"We will be forever grateful to you."

"Thank you, miss, but it's nothing." As he began to walk toward Miss Mary's store, he saw Scipio running toward him, waving an envelope. "Mr. Obi, Mr. Obi, a letter for you." He handed Obi the envelope and then looked at the cabin. "You finish making the school, Mr. Obi? When can I go?"

Miss Fortune smiled at him. "As soon as we have the benches. Do you want to see inside?"

"Oh, yes," he said, excitedly racing ahead of her. Obi sat under one of the oaks to read his letter. It was from Easter.

October 15, 1868

Dear Obi,

I am so sorry to hear about the storm. After I received your letter one came in from Miss Fortune. Obi, she told me that you are rebuilding the school cabin for New Canaan. It is the most wonderful thing you are doing. She also told me that you are helping the other men in New Canaan repair and rebuild cabins. In your last letter you said that there was no decent life for us in New Canaan, but I think New Canaan is the best place for us to be. It seems to me that deep in your heart you know that too. I know you are disappointed about not starting your carpentry business, but you've only been there for a few months. And already you are important to the village.

I believe that all things are possible with God's love, and with our love for each other. Obi right now the village needs you. Rose needs you. You have helped so many people without knowing it. Maybe you don't feel it yet but New Canaan is our home. Why would we want to live anywhere else? We have our own village among our own people. Philadelphia is an interesting city with many things to see and do, but this place will never feel like home to me.

The Fortunes and their friends are taking up a collection of clothes and school supplies to send down to the island. Tell Rose I said not to be so hardheaded and to accept your help. Rose thinks that she is always suppose to do everything herself. She is so prideful. Obi, I want to see you so very much, but I don't want you to use up all of your money just for a trip here. Besides, we are so busy here I might not be able to be with you or see you as often as I would wish. We are busier than ever. We try to make life here like living in a family. I wish I had some sweet grass so that I could show the girls and boys how to make baskets.

Don't waste the money you have to take a trip here. Use that money and time to start another home for us, or to buy more land in New Canaan. Have patience, time is moving quickly. Just know that I love you. Pray that God will keep us safe so that we may be together soon.

Your Easter

He read it twice to fix her voice and her words in his head and carry them in his heart; he still wanted to go to Philadelphia and see her. He kissed the letter and put it in his pocket.

Obi didn't know that Simon and the other boys saw him. "He get a letter from his lady," Simon giggled. "Guess he won't be so hard on us to make the benches just so."

Since the storm, one or two neighbors usually ate with Rose, Obi, and the children. Rose still had a few potatoes and corn in her pantry, and Obi had money to buy food from the supplies and rations sent to the island from the Freedmen's Bureau.

That evening Melissa, who Obi remembered from the Phillips plantation, shared their supper of rice and cow peas. Melissa had lost her chickens, turkeys, and store of corn and potatoes. She brought a small jar of ointment she'd prepared for Grace to rub on Araba's legs—"Make them little bird legs strong."

Melissa left after supper, and Obi read Easter's letter to Rose. Simon's snores filled the cabin while Little Ray and Scipio slept on their pallets next to him. Only Grace and Araba were still awake, with Grace sitting on the rocker, holding Araba and rubbing her thin legs with Melissa's ointment.

When Obi finished, Rose smiled, but her eyes looked tired and her face was drawn. "Why you tell Easter that I won't let you help me?"

"You won't. You worrying about planting cotton again, and getting the money for taxes, when I tell you I'll give you the money for the taxes. You need to let them fields, and yourself, rest."

"You loaning me the money. I planting again, Obi." She paused a moment, fastening her large, dark eyes on Obi. "I don't plan to lay down and die till I dead—not before. I didn't lose my life or my house. I'm blessed. Won't find me sitting here with my hands under my chin propping sorrow."

She stood up and folded her arms across her chest. "You need to start on your cabin, now that you done with the schoolhouse. Easter be here before you turn around twice. And she's right, you know. Y'all don't need to be living nowhere else but here."

He was too tired to argue with Rose. He folded the letter and put it in his back pocket and tried not to think about all of the other letters that had been lost in the storm. Suddenly, there was a light tap on the cabin door.

"Wonder who that is?" Rose asked as she walked to the door. A young black man stood in the dark, softened by the light of a full moon. "Ma'am, I'm looking for a Mr. Booker. The lady in the store say I find him hereabouts."

"I'm Mr. Booker," Obi said as he stepped to the door.

"Mr. Barnwell send me, sir. Sorry for the late hour, but it be a big emergency. Say he want you to make a coffin for the senator."

"Who dead?" Rose asked, ushering the young man into the cabin.

Obi interrupted. "Who's Mr. Barnwell? How he know me?"

"He told me to show you this. Say, he been saving it in case he ever need a carpenter." The young man showed Obi a wrinkled piece of paper. It was the advertisement he'd placed in the paper weeks ago. Obi was surprised. "Who die?"

"The senator."

"What senator?"

"I don't know, sir. Mr. Barnwell just say to come to his house tomorrow morning first thing at Pleasant Point Plantation. You know where it's at?"

"Yes," Obi said. "It's near here, isn't it?"

The young man nodded, but Obi was still perplexed, wondering who the senator was. "Tell him yes."

"I hear a Yankee buy Pleasant Point. Barnwell probably a Yankee man," Rose said.

"Rosie, it look like I have my first real carpenter work. A coffin."

"Poor man. Wonder how he die?" Rose mused.

There was another knock on the door, this time loud and insistent. "What is going on tonight?" Rose said as Obi went to the door.

It was Julius, without his usual politician's grin.

"What happen?" Rose asked. "Come on in and have some tea." She turned to Grace. "Put Araba in the room, Grace, she fast asleep. Then fix Mr. Julius a cup of tea."

For the first time since he'd seen Julius, he looked like the skinny boy he remembered from the plantation. "What's wrong with you?" Obi asked curtly. "Look like the hag ride you all the way here."

"Senator Randolph was killed while he was campaigning in Abbeville County. You remember Senator Randolph, the one I bring to our meeting the night of the storm?"

Rose shuddered and told Julius about the message from Barnwell. Obi wondered, though, why Julius had come. This was the first time since Obi arrived in New Canaan that Julius had shown up at Rose's door.

"Randolph buy property here on Santa Elena. He loved this place. He'll be buried here. They bringing his body tomorrow. It was them Klan did it." His hands shook as Grace gave him the cup. "Found the man swinging from a tree in Abbeville."

"They all dead. They was hanging in the trees. Miss Emma, Mr. George—" Grace's voice startled everyone.

"Grace, you sick? What's the matter?" Rose asked.

Obi was shocked. Grace rarely spoke unless spoken to first. "Forget all of that. You safe now," he said gently.

"Poor thing," Rose muttered. "You go on to sleep. Rest your troubled mind."

"She saw her people hanged," Rose whispered to Julius when Grace had left the room.

Julius sighed. "Almost seem like things be worse since we free." He glanced at Obi, as though trying to draw him into a conversation. Obi recalled how Julius had slighted him at the meeting, but he reminded himself that a man was dead. Someone had taken his life. So he put pettiness behind him.

"You going to keep campaigning?" Obi asked.

He patted his hip. "Yes, long as I have a firearm. But I staying here in Beaufort County." He hesitated a moment. "I would have to have a guard if I went anywhere else. But that's what I was coming here for. We need to start a militia down here. We need men like you, Obi. Men who been soldiers and know about the military."

Obi stared at Julius for a long time, looking through and beyond him. Julius was trying to get his own personal guard. "If the village need men to protect it, then I help long as I'm here. But I ain't joining no militia. I done with military life."

Julius sipped his tea. His hands still trembled slightly. "I understand." His eyes avoided Obi's. "You wanted to talk to me about something the other night? I'm sorry I was busy, and then with the storm, I've been getting in rations from the bureau for the people here . . ." His voice trailed off. Then he cleared his throat. "What was it you wanted to speak to me about?"

"Don't matter now."

Rose spoke up. "Julius, Obi wanted to ask you about carpenter's work. And the next time someone try to speak to you, don't be so high and mighty. You come sliding in here when you scared and think somebody after your hide. That ain't no kind of way to treat folks you been knowing all your life."

Obi had to hold his head down so that Julius didn't see him smile. For a young woman, she sure can fuss like a old hen, he thought.

"I meant no harm, Miss Rose," Julius said, almost childlike. "Obi, you and the other men been doing some good work helping people get their cabins built. If I hear of anyone needing a carpenter, I'll send them to you."

Rose and Julius talked a while longer, and Julius seemed calmer when he left. The smile was back. "I'll see what I can do for you, Obi," he said.

Before Obi went to sleep on the pallet Rose had made for him with an old quilt, he wrote a letter to Easter.

October 26, 1868

Dear Easter,

I received your letter today and I'm happy to know that you are fine. All the things you say are right and make good sense. But Easter, I don't care if it's for one day or only one moment. I must lay my eyes on your sweet face. No place is home unless you're with me. You and Jason. Can't you understand that? All of these many years we are apart, I have been living and doing what I must, but I am use to doing that. Doing what I have been told to do. I was a slave. All slaves do what they told. That's why we make good soldiers. Nobody knows what's inside a slave's soul.

What does it matter if I build a school cabin or a hut for someone who lost their home. I do it because it needs to be done. I hate to see people suffer because I know how suffering hurts. But then, I get angry. And I begin to hate this mean little ugly mud hole. But my heart, my feelings be a separate thing from a cabin or this place. The only time my heart and my actions was one thing, was when I began to build our home, because as I hammered and sawed, I see you sitting on the porch or looking out of a window.

Well, Easter, I hope that you don't think I've lost my wits. I am only trying to tell you how I feel. But words alone cannot express the deep feelings in my heart, especially for you.

I have carpentry work, but it is for a sad reason. I have to make a coffin for a Senator who was killed. Someone have to die before I get paying carpenter's work. Do not be surprised if you see me at your doorstep for Christmas.

Love, your Obi

13

The strong men keep a-comin' on
The strong men git stronger.
—*STERLING BROWN*

"Mister Booker, where did you learn to do work like this?" Jonathan Barnwell stared at the cedar coffin Obi had just completed. "You are truly an artisan."

Obi leaned against the work table in the large carpenter's shed. He had never heard the word *artisan* before, but he supposed that it was a nice compliment. "When I was a slave. I learn from the slave carpenter I was apprentice to."

"The family will be pleased. I know it. He was a good man. We were friends."

Obi had been surprised that morning when he'd arrived at Pleasant Point, the 300-acre plantation owned by Jonathan Barnwell. Barnwell, a Yankee, was the same white man he'd seen at their Friday meeting when Senator Randolph spoke.

"Mister Booker, I would love to have you to work for me, but I only need field hands now." He gazed at the laborers in the gathering dusk. "When I need a carpenter, I will call you."

This was the most respectful white man Obi had ever met. The ten dollars he'd made replaced the money he'd given Rose—a lot of money for one day's work. "I do all kind of carpenter's work, sir. I make furniture as well."

"Mr. Booker, I promise you will be hearing from me again. I appreciate a man who works the way you do. You even have your own tools. Very businesslike, young man. Very businesslike."

"Thank you, sir," Obi said. *And thank you, Miss Fortune, for letting me borrow these tools.* They shook hands.

As Obi walked back to New Canaan's "hub"—the church, the store, and the new school—he felt somewhat lifted up, but he knew that a handshake and a promise didn't mean he was close to getting his own business. And a man had to die for him to get work.

It was completely dark when Obi reached the school. He took the latch off the door and put the tools behind the woodstove. Tomorrow he'd build a small toolshed. Squinting in the dark, Obi tried to see whether Simon and the other boys had made the benches as he'd told them to do. He felt around in the dark and ran his hands over the surface of two bumpy objects. He sucked his teeth in disgust. *Little Scipio do better than this.*

He left the school cabin and went to Miss Mary's store.

"Hello, Mr. Booker. Got some mail for you. Just getting ready to close up. Didn't see you today. You're done with the school, eh?" She didn't wait for him to answer. "Them boys was in the schoolhouse, making the benches. Mr. Booker, they can't do nothing without you. I walked over there to see how they getting on, and my lord, them benches crooked as a winding road."

"I know, Miss Mary. I'll help them tomorrow."

"Whose house you working on now? Saw Samuel and James, said they patching up Melissa's cabin. This a time, yes, Mr. Obi?"

She put the basket on the counter. He rummaged through the envelopes and found a letter from Thomas. He couldn't think of a better time to hear from his old friend. "Miss Mary, can I read this by the light of your lantern?"

"Of course, Mr. Booker. Must be important, since you can't wait till you get home to read it."

September 30, 1868

Hello Cpl. Booker,

I hope this letter finds you well. I hope this letter finds you. As for Peter and I, we are having a grand time. Obi, we are truly sorry that you are not with us. What adventures we've had. First, we bought ourselves a new set of clothing and luggage fit for gentlemen like ourselves. However, in order to pose as fine gentlemen I had to tell Peter not to speak. For when he's done mangling the King's English then people know that we are frauds. But here in New Orleans, the steamers bring in frauds everyday.

We arrived in New Orleans a few days after we left you in Beaufort, and we have been here ever since. There is a joyfulness here that I have not seen elsewhere—not even in New York. The blacks and whites mingle freely. They ride in the same streetcars and can go to the same places of amusement, as long as they have the money to spend. The most beautiful colored and mulatto women I've ever seen are here. They put the New York and Charleston girls to shame.

People speak mostly French, and everyday is a festive occasion. Also, there is no sabbath on Sundays. I mean by that—people are in the streets buying and selling goods. Music and dancing are everywhere. It is hard to imagine when I look around that only a few months ago colored people were hunted and shot down like mad dogs in the street. Maybe politics and power make men wild.

We will be leaving this glorious city tomorrow. I hope that we do not have trouble getting passsage. Some of these steamboat captains refuse to take Black passengers. We will take the steamer to St. Louis and then work our way to Kansas. We hear that there's plenty of land there. We'll save some for you.

When we're settled in we'll send you our address so that you can write to us. Watch out for stray rebels.

Sincerely,
Your friend Thomas Smith

Obi carefully folded the letter and put it back in the envelope. As he walked down the shelled road, he began to seriously consider the idea of settling in the West with Easter and Jason.

November brought more rain and dampness and the illness that always follows bad weather. Yet New Canaan tried to recover from the storm. November was also the time to vote. Neither rain nor threats from employers kept Obi and the other men of New Canaan from voting on election day. Julius lost his bid for a seat on the state legislature but retained his appointment on the South Carolina Land Commission.

Obi spent all of his time helping the village men throw up shacks as fast as they could and helping Rose clear her land and patch up her cabin. Simon worked with them in the afternoons when he returned from school. During the days of endless labor, Rose and Obi continued to badger one another. "Obi, you need to start working on your house again," she would say.

And he'd say to her, "Rosie, you need to forget about these cotton fields and rent your land." Neither one of them had a change of heart.

By the end of November he received a package and a letter from Easter.

November 15, 1868

Dear Obi,

    I hope that you, Rose and everyone are fine after all of your troubles. I am so sorry that we will not be able to spend Christmas together. I made inquiries about the possibility of time off for the holidays, but I was told that wouldn't be possible. We have an extra crowd of children from men and women both who are raising children alone and have no one to care for them while they work. Also the cold weather forces many poor people to leave their children with us. We are full to overflowing, but will try to make as nice a Christmas for them as possible.

    Obi, I want very much to see you as well, but it doesn't make sense to spend that money and we won't be together as much as we would like to be. It would hurt me terribly knowing that you are here in Philadelphia and I cannot see you. Your letter was so loving, but sad. I've read it many times, and I think that you are becoming discouraged. Obi, a hate-filled heart only sees meanness and ugliness. Please do not be. Begin building our new home and our new life. Have patience, Obi. One day soon we will be side by side in New Canaan.

    I have sent some things for all of you, including the children. Miss Fortune's family collected clothing and supplies to send to the freed people, as they say up here in the North. I asked the family whether I could pick out a few things to send to you all from the clothing they collected. I hope that the clothing fit the young ones. I wrote to Miss Fortune asking her to describe the children's sizes to me. Sorry that none of this clothing is new, but everything is in fine condition. (I was a little extravagant Obi and bought something new for you.)

    I am busy as always between work at the orphanage and school. Well, forgive these secondhand gifts, but they come from my heart.

I wish I could be there with you all. Love to everyone. I will write again soon.

Your Easter

P.S. Here is an address for Jason. He goes by the last name Jennings. He says he will be here for a good spell. He's performing in a theater in Chicago, in the big city!

Write to him in care of: Bliden's Theatre, 420 Dearborn Street, Chicago, Illinois.

Obi opened his gift—a well-crafted wooden box filled with paper, ink, and pen nibs. He wrote her back immediately.

November 30, 1868

Dear Easter,

I hope that you are well. I was happy to get your letter and to get Jason's address. I am going to write him tonight also. Thank you for the writing box, papers, etc. I am making immediate use of it. The children will be so excited over the clothing. Next month the transport is coming here, and I will send them on to the Refugee camp. For now, they are happy.

Everything you say makes good sense, Easter, but I am still coming up there for Christmas, or a few days afterward. I cannot wait. I must see you if only for a few moments. In the meantime, I am use to doing what I am told (laugh). You tell me to wait so I will but only after I have laid my eyes on you once more. Then I will come back here and wait for you. But Easter I am still not sure about the kind of future we would have here in New Canaan. I still have not made progress on my own carpentry business. I thought I might get more carpentry work from the Yankee who hired me to make the coffin for the Senator who was killed, but he has not contacted me again.

I have heard from my army friends who are settling in the West. Easter, I think it is something we should consider when you return. My friends tell me there is land in the West, and a much better life than here in the South. In the meantime, I have plenty to do helping the other men. The next important thing is getting Jason back down here. Then when we are all three together we can see whether we can make our plans.

I love you, Easter. Write back soon.

Your Obi

Then Obi wrote to Jason.

Dear Jason,

I cannot believe that I have finally caught up to you and you are settled in one place where you can get a letter. I hope you are well. I guess that you are no longer the skinny boy in shirttails. Easter has told me you have been in a medicine show, and now you are in a theatre. Well, Jason you was always a good singer and dancer and full of fun, but that is no kind of life for a boy, to be knocking about in tent shows and minstrel shows.

Easter and I will become husband and wife, and Jason, though there is no blood between us, you are like our child and you must be with us and we all live together. We three are lucky that we find each other. We should never live separate again. Jason, come to New Canaan soon. Easter will be back down here in the Spring and we will be married. And the three of us can begin our lives as a family. We don't have to stay here on this island, or even in the

South, though Easter wants to. Perhaps we will move to the West.
Wherever we move to, we want you with us. You belong with us.

Love, Obi

For the first time in a long time, Obi felt almost complete, having written to Easter and Jason all in one night.

14

*We were waked early by the people knocking at our
window and shouting "Merry Christmas."*

—*CHARLOTTE FORTEN,* THE JOURNALS OF
CHARLOTTE FORTEN GRIMKE

December 1868

The fifty children of the New Canaan School stood proudly before
their families and neighbors on a Sunday afternoon a little over a week
before Christmas. The day was unusually warm and sunny, as though
in their honor. As Obi sat down on the bench, he realized that this was
the first time he'd been in church for anything other than the Friday-
evening Republican meetings.

Miss Fortune and her students had decorated the pulpit with ever-
green wreaths, and the newly whitewashed walls with garlands of moss
and sprigs of holly. The children themselves were washed and
scrubbed, and everyone had managed to wear a white shirt or blouse,
as Miss Fortune had asked them to do. Some had newer clothing than
others; many of the clothes were either too big or too small, obviously
donations from the missionaries.

Obi, Rose, and Grace sat near the front, and Scipio smiled brightly.
He and Simon stood with their schoolmates. Little Ray wanted to stand

with them and was only satisfied when Rose took him off her lap and let him and Araba sit on the floor.

Miss Fortune stood before the audience. She too wore a white blouse with ruffles down the front and a dark skirt. "Ladies and gentlemen, the children of New Canaan proudly present their Christmas program to you. They have worked so very hard and learned so much in just a few weeks of school, without books and slates, paper and pens, with only their hearts and wills. They present these songs and poems to you with joy and love." She gazed around the audience as though searching for someone. Then she said, "Had it not been for Mr. Booker, they would not even have had a building to go into." She smiled and clapped, and all eyes turned on him. Someone in the audience said, "Amen! A fine job." Obi wanted to slide under the bench.

Rose chuckled. "You definitely one of us now."

Miss Fortune turned around and faced the children with both arms upraised. And when every child's eye rested on her, she held her arms higher, stabbing the air with her hands. Instantly, the children's voices filled the church with a pure sound. Scipio's voice could be heard loud and clear over the others, reminding Obi of the way Jason used to sing.

Hold your light, Brother
Hold your light,
Hold your light on Canaan's shore.

What make ole Satan for follow me so?
Satan's got nothing to do with me.
Hold your light,
Hold your light,
Hold your light on Canaan's shore.

They sang other songs, and the audience clapped and sang with them. Rose whispered to Obi, "Look how Grace is smiling. I never see her smile so. And see how the stiff Miss Fortune swaying from side to side. Guess she ain't altogether Yankee."

Obi laughed. "Look at Araba," he said. She and Little Ray bounced vigorously. "I never see her move this much." He was amazed too at what Miss Fortune had accomplished with the children in such a short time. With nothing but her and the children's willing and hopeful spirits. She had a comfortable home in Philadelphia to go back to, he thought. *Yet she stay in this mudhole, and look what she did.*

Scipio's starring moment interrupted Obi's thoughts. Miss Fortune faced the audience again. "And now a recitation by one of our newest and youngest students. Scipio Booker will recite 'Bury Me in a Free Land,' by Frances Ellen Harper." Obi was surprised. He never told Miss Fortune that Scipio's last name was Booker.

Scipio stepped before the audience, shoulders straight, eyes bright, and in a loud clear voice began:

Make me a grave where'er you will,
In a lowly plain or a lofty hill;

Scipio raised his arms dramatically.

Make it among earth's humblest graves,
But not in a land where men are slaves.

I ask no monument proud and high,
To arrest the gaze of the passers by;

All that my yearning spirit craves
Is, Bury me not in a Land of Slaves.

The audience clapped loudly while Scipio, placing one arm behind his back and the other across his stomach, bowed deeply. And before Rose could catch him, Little Ray scrambled up to the front and bowed with Scipio. The church erupted in laughter. Obi couldn't remember the last time he laughed so hard. Rose started to go after Ray, but Obi pulled her back. "He just a baby."

She relaxed when Miss Fortune smiled too and gently patted Little Ray on the head, as he continued to bow and the audience laughed and cheered him on too. Suddenly Grace yanked his arm and shouted, "Mr. Obi, Miss Rose, look Araba." Araba stood up on her thin wobbly legs and, holding onto the seat of the bench, moved one foot before the other and took several steps before falling back down. Grace reached to pick her up, but Rose stopped her. Araba stood up again and took a few more steps. Obi shook his head in disbelief. "Araba's walking."

Rose clasped her hands. "It like a miracle, Obi. Look at that."

Everyone in the church remarked on how "that child just upped and walked," though Araba did more wobbling than walking. She wobbled, fell, laughed, and picked herself up again and again and yet again.

"She never stay down," Obi laughed as he watched her trying to keep up with Little Ray and the other children as they left the church.

Two days after the Christmas program, as he and Rose cleared the last pieces of debris from her fields, Obi spotted Simon running toward them. He only went to school in the morning and helped Rose and Obi in the afternoon.

"Mr. Obi, Miss Mary sent this. She say it look important."

"Lord, that woman is nosy," Rose mumbled as she looked over Obi's shoulder. "Is it from Easter?"

He shook his head as he tore the envelope open. "It's from the bureau."

Obi read the letter and then turned to Rose. "A transport will be coming to the island on December twentieth at seven A.M. I could put the children on it, and they would be taken to Edisto Island with a group of other refugees."

If the children left on the twentieth, he'd book passage on a ship going to Philadelphia and might get there by Christmas or a few days after, he thought to himself, but said nothing to Rose. He dared not.

Rose sat down on a fallen log. "I got use to having them around. So sad, Obi, just a few days before Christmas. That little Araba. She falling more than she walking, but she won't let nobody pick her up. Not even Grace."

"Whenever they leave, it will be sad, Rose. It has to be done sometime. Can you take care of them? Can I?"

"We been taking care of them."

"But that's not how it was supposed to be, Rose. You have enough here to take care of. And me and Easter don't even have a roof over our heads."

She looked at him sharply. "Whose fault that be?" She stood up and picked up a clump of branches and leaves, throwing them in the pile for burning. "Obi, only God know what's suppose to be. Keep telling you, man proposes and God disposes. When you going to tell Grace?"

Rose was giving him a headache. "In time, Rose. No point in upsetting her too soon."

"So you going to just tell them five minutes before you throw them on the ship?"

Obi sucked his teeth loudly. "No."

When they returned to the cabin before dark, Araba wobbled over to Obi so that he could pick her up and swoop her in the air and then put her down. Then she wobbled over to Rose and Simon. This was a new ritual. Little Ray followed, even imitating the way Araba walked.

Grace had started roasting the potatoes on the fireplace. "Miss Rose, these are the last of the potatoes left in the pantry."

"I know. Well, least we had a good store, last us a few months."

Obi turned to Grace. "Come outside a moment, I have to talk to you." Simon glanced sadly at Grace and then Obi. Rose handed Grace a shawl. "Here, put this on. It's chilly and damp."

Obi could tell that Grace knew what he was going to say. As soon as they stepped outside, she lowered her face. "Grace, the transport will be here tomorrow, it's time now. I wish we could keep you, but we can't. Miss Rose lose all her crop, and I . . ." He couldn't continue. He hated the sound of his voice. He tilted her chin. Her eyes were blank.

"Grace? You understand what I'm telling you?"

She lowered her head again. "Yes, Mr. Obi, but I thought we was staying with you."

Obi's head throbbed. "I explained this to you before, Grace. The missionaries will take good care of you and Araba and Scipio."

After they went back inside Rose whispered, "When you telling Scipio?"

"Tomorrow is soon enough."

15

I want to go to Canaan,
To meet the coming day.
—*AFRICAN AMERICAN SPIRITUAL*

After an uneasy, fitful sleep, Obi woke up before everyone else. He drew water from the well for the morning tea and started the fire. After making himself a cup of tea, he sat at the table. Obi lit a candle and finished carving the small wooden sailboat he'd been making for Scipio's Christmas present. He'd already purchased a dress for each of the girls from Miss Fortune's supply of donated clothing.

When Obi finished the sailboat, he polished the wood with beeswax. He turned it around in his hand and admired its perfect small shape. Obi hoped that someday the children would understand—he'd kept them for as long as he could. As he wrapped the boat and the dresses together in brown paper, Scipio woke up.

"Morning, Mr. Obi."

"Morning, Scipio. You rest a spell longer. It's not day clean yet."

"Miss Fortune don't like us to be late for school."

"You not . . . you not going to . . . to be late for school."

"And you know what, Mr. Obi?" He jumped off the pallet and bounced over to the table. "I has a secret to tell you."

"What?"

He cupped his hands over his mouth and whispered directly in

Obi's ear. "We making Christmas pictures in school. Miss Fortune has a big box of colors and papers from the North. I'm making a picture for Miss Rose. It the best one in the class."

"That's nice . . . that's nice."

"And you know what else, Mr. Obi? That box you made me with all the money I been saving? I buying candy oranges for Grace and Araba and gumdrops for Simon and Little Ray." Then he smiled mischievously. "Can't tell what I giving you, Mr. Obi, then it wouldn't be no surprise." Scipio's bright eyes scanned the package. "What's that, Mr. Obi?"

"Scipio, you go on and clean your face, since you ain't going back to sleep."

Scipio bounded over to Simon. "Get up, Simon. Time for school!"

"You just go and take care of your business. I'll wake Simon up."

As Obi went about the rest of his morning routine, he only wished that all of this were over and done with. By the time dawn had broken through the dark sky, everyone was awake, except Little Ray.

Rose walked into the main room. Grace followed her, carrying Araba as she'd done in the past instead of letting her walk on her own. And Araba didn't resist and squirm. As if she too knew that something was different—wasn't right. Rose picked up Little Ray and carried him, still asleep, into her room. She didn't want him to wake up and cry after the children when they left.

While Scipio sparkled and chattered on about the school play, Grace, sitting next to him on the bench, stared into space—something she rarely did when they were all inside the house together.

Rose's face was stern but her voice soft and her eyes sad as she gazed at Grace and Scipio. "Stop all that talk and eat your grits before they get cold. And Grace, you know we don't waste food around here. Eat. Can't go out there with a empty belly."

Rose reached for Araba. "I'll feed her. You eat."

Obi sat down on the bench opposite them. "Grace, you listen to Miss Rose. You have to eat something."

Grace picked up her spoon and slowly, without appetite, ate as she was told to do.

Suddenly Scipio realized that something was not right. "Grace, what's wrong with you?"

She didn't answer, so he turned to Obi. "What's wrong with Grace?"

"Nothing. You go on and eat now."

His smiling cheery face disappeared. "Why Araba all dressed up? Where she going?" His eyes darted from Rose to Obi. "Where's Simon? Ain't he going to school too?"

"He just went to take care of his business, Scipio. Now, don't you worry," Obi said.

"Why is Little Ray in the bedroom? Ain't he going to play with Araba today?"

"Scipio, it's time now. You have to go with the missionaries," Obi said.

"You coming too? And Miss Rose, and Little Ray and Simon?"

"We'll visit you, all of us." Obi glanced at Rose. She couldn't help him.

Scipio frowned, until he understood. Then he cried. "Mr. Booker, you sending us away? You not coming too? Please let us stay with you and Miss Rose. Why you cross with us? I'll be good."

Obi put an arm around his shoulders. "Come now. You too big a boy to be crying like a baby. We'll visit you."

Araba looked up from Rose's lap, saw Scipio's tears, and began to whimper. Grace's eyes were blank.

"I keep them," Rose said.

Obi stood up. "How? You can hardly keep yourself."

She couldn't argue that point. Rose kissed Scipio on his forehead.

"You hush now, Scipio. You ain't going to be that far from us, and we will visit you soon." She wrapped Araba's blue blanket around her shoulders. "It's raw out there this morning. You have to keep warm." She kissed and hugged Araba and kissed the top of Grace's head. Rose walked back into the bedroom so that she wouldn't have to see them leave. Simon didn't come back into the cabin, but watched sadly from the fields as Obi and the three children walked down the path coated with light frost.

Obi held the children's package in one hand and Scipio's hand in the other. Grace carried Araba, and Obi was certain that the child knew. She let Grace carry her without a fuss. Scipio tried hard not to cry.

Signs of the storm were still strewn alongside the shelled road—the praise house was a pile of boards, and downed trees lay like broken statues, no longer forming a leafy ceiling. When Obi passed Miss Mary's store, he saw gray swirls of smoke curling out of the chimney. He had a sudden urge to go inside and smell the scent of nutmeg, lemon, and honey and drink a cup of warm tea. Scipio's eyes were big and wet as he spotted the school cabin behind the church. Obi was glad that it was too early and Miss Fortune wasn't in front of the schoolhouse greeting her students.

When they reached the dock, there were a few military people waiting for the transport. It wasn't long before Obi saw a distant shadow in the mists rising from the water. By the time the ship reached them and began to dock, the children were shivering. Obi made sure that Scipio's jacket was buttoned. Then he adjusted Grace's shawl on her shoulders and checked that Araba's blanket was tight and secure.

Obi and the children remained at the end of the line of passengers waiting to board. As the boat docked, he wondered how many refugees it carried. Were they as desperate and ragged as the people he'd seen during the war or the people he'd helped when he served at the Freedmen's Bureau? He gazed at the children. What was he sending them into? Was there anyone on the ship who could comfort them? Would other children take their possessions when they reached the camp? Were there any women there as kind as Rose who would care for them and help them? Would Araba continue to walk? Would Grace ever smile?

The crewmen let down the gangplank, and people began to board the ship. Obi followed slowly, and as he drew near, he had a sinking feeling in the pit of his stomach. His head throbbed. It seemed to him that the ship was packed. What would happen to Scipio, Araba, and Grace?

"Hey you, hurry up. We don't have all day," one of the crewmen yelled at him.

He looked into the man's hard little face, and he couldn't do it. He couldn't send them on that ship. Obi turned around. "Come on, y'all," he said to them, taking Scipio's hand.

Scipio, still fighting tears, asked, "Where we going?"

"Home."

"Obi, I know in the end you do what's right," Rose said as she threw a large tree branch in the fire Obi had started. They were burning the few remaining dead leaves and branches left over from the storm.

"Seem cruel to send them away now just before Christmas. That camp ain't going nowhere. I can take them anytime."

"They belong here, Obi. In New Canaan." Rose threw another branch in the fire, and it blazed for a moment. "You know Obi, there's nothing more precious than a child's love."

Obi picked up a small log and threw it in the fire. "Still, nothing is settled."

Rose wiped her forehead. The stinging rain had given way to warm sunlight. "The only time things be settled is when you dead in your grave. You good and settled then. You know it would be a cruel thing to throw them children on a boat and send them away like that."

He agreed. Everyone and everything was back in place. Scipio was back in school and helping Miss Mary in the afternoon. He bounced like a little ball when he delivered a letter to Obi later that day. Grace's eyes were no longer blank as she cleaned and watched Araba and Little Ray and helped Rose prepare dinner. Araba and Little Ray played together. In their world nothing had ever changed. As they sat around the table together, Obi felt as though he had completed a long journey.

He read Easter's letter that evening after everyone was asleep.

December 4, 1868

Dearest Obi,

This is to wish you and Rose and all of the Children a Blessed Christmas. You are determined to come here, so I can't stop you, but I wish you would think again. As much as I want to see you, it seems as if it's such a waste of money if we can't spend time together. The orphanage is so full and crowded, but the children are happy in spite of all. As Christmas draws near, my thoughts go home, thinking of the past Christmases we spent together. Remember how Jennings would let us go to the Phillips Plantation, and even you danced a reel once, and Jason was just crazy out of his wits with dancing and singing. Obi, please try and think of New Canaan as our home even in hard times. You know, New Canaan is the place where I became free. When I think of the island and our little village it reminds me of the times we spent with the other slaves on the Phillips Plantation. Oh yes, we were slaves on the outside, but we were people too on the inside. As you said in your letter, who knows what is in the heart of a slave. We knew what was in each other's hearts. We all had to be there to look within one another. You, me, Rose, Rayford and all of the other slaves. We have to be where people truly see us, and know us. I believe so deeply in my heart that there can be no place safer or better for us. So I only want you to try again. Build again.

Well, I hope you don't think I'm a mad woman. Just missing you and loving you and hoping you're not growing too impatient with me.

Your Easter

Obi reread the letter several times, so that he'd remember her words. Later on that evening, when everything was quiet except for Simon's snoring, Obi answered Easter's letter.

December 20, 1868

Dear Easter,

Rose and everyone send their hellos. Your letters bring me great comfort and joy. I have some news for you. Today, I was supposed to send Grace, Araba and Scipio to the camp, but I could not bring myself to do it. And so they are still here with me and Rose. I have made a decision as concerns them. I will have to keep them until I can find the right situation for them here. Rose wanted to keep them all along. But Rose cannot take in any more children. I brought them here, so they are my responsibility for now. I will have to wait here for your return as you wanted me to do in the first place.

Easter, I will try once again to build a life for us here because that is what you wish. I am even going to behave as the other people here do, and ask the men to help me. However, nothing will feel right inside or outside of me until we are together. I will try to be hopeful, but it is hard. It seems as though every time I feel a bit of joy, something happens.

By the way, I am waiting to hear from Jason, still. I wonder if he received the letter I sent to him. Maybe he's afraid to write me back. Thinks that I will snatch him out of that theater and bring him with me—where he belongs. Then both of us can come to your doorstep, Easter. (laugh) Wouldn't that be a time? Anyway, my love, that is all for now. Write back soon.

Your Obi

16

The little baby gone home,
The little baby gone along,
For to climb up Jacob's ladder.
—*AFRICAN AMERICAN SPIRITUAL*

January 2, 1869

"That spring weather was a fooler yesterday," Samuel said as he and Obi watched the tree they'd just sawed fall to the ground. "You know, this a good time to put up a cabin. Before the spring planting." Samuel began to saw the branches off the tree. "We have this cabin up in a couple of days if Brother Paul and James get over here like they promise."

Obi picked up the other handsaw. He was still borrowing tools from Miss Fortune, but promised to begin to buy himself new tools again the next time he earned money from carpentry work. "I think more than a couple of days, Samuel. We have to build another foundation. When Simon come this afternoon, I going to start him mixing the sand and shell—"

"Use logs for the foundation."

"The tabby looks better," Obi said as he sawed the thick branches.

"Look better? You painting a picture or building a house to keep your hide out of the rain?"

"I want the house to be pretty like a picture and still keep me and Easter warm and dry."

"I thought since you're not buying logs this time that you just building a simple cabin."

"I am. But it has to look in a pleasant way. Now I'm going to show you how to cure the wood so it fit just right in the joints. We make a rack and a cover and build a small fire under the wood and—"

"When is Easter coming home?" Samuel interrupted Obi's explanation.

"In May."

"This one or the next?"

"I ain't having no jimmy swing cabin with logs piled up on each other and a tiny space for door and window."

"Yes, but you want to get it up before the woman come home looking for a place to lay her head, Obi. You work a man harder than any slave master I ever know."

Samuel threw the branches he'd cut into a pile of other leaves. "Look like we getting some more help, Obi."

Obi looked in the direction of Rose's cabin and saw Julius walking toward them. He sucked his teeth. "You a big jokester, Samuel. You know Julius ain't coming here to dirty his hands." Especially building my house, he added to himself.

Julius wore a finely made gray linen jacket with a waistcoat to match and a well-cut pair of trousers.

Samuel spoke first. "Brother Obi, I think Julius come to tell you why he can't help you today."

Julius ignored him. "We having a important meeting of the Beaufort Republican Club tomorrow, so I have to go there."

"You walk over here to tell us that?"

"No. I have a message from your wife. When I walk past your house she ask me to tell you to stop by Miss Mary store and buy syrup for your little girl. Say Charlotte still have that cough."

Samuel wiped his forehead. "That woman keep a man busy." He smiled slightly, and Obi knew that a joke was coming. "Keep two men busy. Have an important man like Julius bringing me a message."

"I always willing to help," Julius said. "Now you help me and make sure you come to the next meeting."

"Julius, don't start speechifying. We have work to do. Obi needs a cabin," Samuel said.

"This political work just as important as the work you doing." Julius had tried to be cordial to Obi ever since the night he came to Rose's cabin, but Obi could tell it took all of Julius's politician's skill to be friendly. "Obi, Samuel, I talk to you about this too. I still want us to form a militia on this island."

"Be glad to," Samuel said. "After I done building Obi's cabin and planting and harvesting and making up for what I lost last year. The militia paying wages?"

"I told you before, Julius. I help protect the village, but I ain't joining no militia," Obi said. "I finish with army life."

"You men think about it. You remember Jonathan Barnwell, the one you did that work for, Obi? He move back to Massachusetts. Sell his land to another Yankee couple. The Klan threaten him when he was in Edgefield, registering voters."

"Well, he shoulda stay down here with us. Ain't no Klan here," Samuel said before Obi could answer.

Julius waved as he walked away. "See you at the next meeting. Think about what I say. All the other men are joining."

Julius left, and Samuel smiled slowly as if savoring his own joke first before he told it to anyone else. He pointed to Julius in the distance. "He the biggest Republican since Lincoln die. They say the president use to split log when he a boy. Julius better split these logs, and maybe he be president some day. I ain't got time for no militia. I already have my rifle, any Klan worry me."

Several other men came later on in the day to help them. They cut down more trees, and Obi tried to keep doubts at bay and maintain the good spirits he'd begun the day with. But it was hard to do. His one possibility for carpentry work had been run out of South Carolina. Still, Obi decided to put another ad in the Santa Elena paper.

"They even running white men away from here. What chance for the likes of us?" Obi said to Samuel as he walked with him to Miss Mary's store before dusk.

"Well, all these Republicans and politicians and Yankees need to stay away from them upstate places. Them Democrats and Red Shirts ain't going to rest till they run all of us out of there. Obi, me and you is alike. All I want is to care for my family and for us to be safe and to live well, and for my little girl to get good schooling. Someday grow up to be a educated young woman, like your Easter. She and Easter be good friends, you know."

When they neared the store, Samuel said, "I told my wife to get the missionary doctor, Dr. Emmy, we call her, the one who work with Miss Fortune. I don't think this conjure syrup from Miss Mary be enough. Charlotte need real medicine."

"People get colds. Especially the children. Charlottte look like a healthy girl," Obi said.

Samuel frowned and rubbed his forehead. "Last year a lot of children had that bad whooping cough and die."

"Most of the children who die from the whooping cough are infants." Obi remembered reading an article about whooping cough in a newspaper once—when he was first learning how to read. "Your girl be about five or six years. It doesn't do them as bad."

Samuel tried to brighten. "She's a big strong gal, like her mama. She'll be all right. I get that syrup and the doctor medicine too."

After Samuel purchased the cough syrup and Obi checked the mail, they walked back down the shelled road together. "Sam, tomorrow I show you how to cure them logs."

"You a taskmaster. See you after day clean. I ain't coming out in the dark of dawn like you."

Patches of daylight were appearing in the dark sky when Obi left Rose's cabin the following morning. He thought he saw a figure walking toward him, but he wasn't certain. Until the person drew near. Samuel. *Something terrible happen.* Samuel wouldn't walk to Rose's to meet him. He'd go directly to the unfinished cabin.

"My baby die last night, Obi. Can you make she a coffin?" His voice trembled, and his usually smiling round face sagged.

Obi had never made a child's coffin before. "This be sorrowful work," he said to Simon, who had offered to help him. All the while he worked he recalled how Charlotte would come into the yard to play with Little Ray and the other children—even with Grace, who didn't play.

People remarked at the beauty of the coffin Obi had made, as if such a thing could be beautiful. He smoothed the wood, polished it with beeswax, and carved a heart with her name written underneath, along with the dates of her birth and death. Samuel tried to pay him, but Obi refused to take his money. "You been a friend to me."

Charlotte was buried the following evening in the cemetery behind the church. They sang "The Baby Gone Home" while Samuel's wails shattered the night. Charlotte's mother, Laura, placed the girl's treasured doll on her grave—a store-bought doll, not the corn husk dolls that most of the girls played with. She did not cry. "Most of these women's tears dry up long ago," Rose whispered to Obi as Brother Paul began to pray.

When Obi raised his head after the prayer, Grace was holding Araba tightly, as she used to do before Araba had started walking. And instead of squirming, Araba held on to Grace. Later on that evening Scipio begged Obi to let him sleep next to him on his pallet.

"Why?" Obi asked.

"I afraid."

"You be okay. Nothing happen to you. I'm right here. Simon's here, and so is Little Ray."

While Simon, Scipio, and Little Ray lay across their pallets, and Rose and the girls slept in the other room, Obi wrote Easter a short, sad letter about Charlotte's death.

January 4, 1869

My Dearest Easter,

I am sorry to have to tell you this bad news, but your little friend Charlotte has died. Someone told me that she was one of the first children you taught. Well, the poor little girl was buried to-night. I had the sad task of making her coffin. Her father, Samuel, has been a friend to me, so I tried to make it as beautiful as you could make such a sad thing. She had that whooping cough. It seems as though many children are falling ill. The weather has turned so cold, and many people still do not have enough food, fuel and the right kind of shelter. Rose is worried about keeping the children we have here healthy. So far we are all well. I know that you are busy so I won't give you too much to read.

I miss you very much. I still have no word from Jason.

Love, Obi

17

Early in the year one of my little scholars died.
—ELIZABETH HYDE BOTUME, TEACHER, FREEDMEN'S SCHOOL

Charlotte was only the beginning. The damp, cold, rain-drenched days of January brought many other deaths—especially for children. Each time Obi thought that he would continue working on his cabin, he had to make a tiny coffin instead. People from other parts of the island came to him. They'd heard of the young carpenter in New Canaan who'd made a beautiful coffin for the senator who had been killed, and for a little New Canaan girl.

He was paid with chickens, eggs, fish, boots from a man who knew the cobbler's trade, and a pair of well-cut trousers made out of good broadcloth.

Obi continued to attend the New Canaan Republican Club every Friday evening. On an unusually cold and rainy Friday, when he returned to Rose's cabin after a meeting, Araba was whimpering, cradled in Rose's arms.

"What happen?" Obi asked.

"Just a cold, but we ain't taking no chances. You better take some tea too. You wet from the rain. Look at you, Obi."

Rose daubed the child's forehead with a damp cloth. "It's all right, baby," she cooed. "You rest." She rocked her in her arms.

Grace handed him a cup of tea, her face haggard and haunted

again. Obi touched Araba's forehead with the back of his hand. "She have a fever."

"Only slight. But I not waiting for her to get sick. Give her some of this tea, and that keep the cold from getting worse."

The next morning he was relieved to see Araba struggling over to him, determined to walk on her own, so that he could swoop her in the air as he'd done every morning since she'd started walking. Little Ray held his hands up for his ride through the air too.

"The weather dampish," Rose said, "and she seem to have a slight fever still, but Grace will be with her while I begin to work on the kitchen garden."

"Melissa brewing her up some sassafras root and some soup. I might even ask the missionary doctor to look at her. She'll be fine," Rose assured him.

Obi opened the door. "I'm going to Elenaville to put another carpenter's ad in the paper. When I return, I'll be working on my cabin."

"Be careful, don't snatch up any more white men in the collar," Rose chuckled as Obi left.

The evergreens sparkled in the warm sunlight, so different from the rainy cold night before. A clear, fresh, hopeful morning.

Obi placed the identical ad in the paper that he'd put there before. However, this time he wrote it out beforehand. When he stepped into the newspaper office, the same man sat behind the receptionist's desk. "I'm placing this ad for five weeks," Obi said, putting the paper and five dollars on the desk.

The man picked it up, read it, and said, "Thank Mr. Booker for us."

Obi smiled to himself as he left the office. If the newspaper man didn't remember him, he doubted anyone else would. *Can't tell one of us from the other.* Instead of going back to New Canaan, he walked to the end of the street. There were remnants of the storm in Elenaville too. Some trees were down, and others were bent in the direction the wind had taken. The houses, however, seemed to have withstood nature's fury better than the cabins and lean-tos on other parts of the island.

He gazed at the house girded with the two porches, his favorite of all of the homes sitting on the bluff, and imagined Easter promenading around the porch of a house like that one. Perhaps he'd try again, especially if he got more carpentry work. He could put up the cabin temporarily, and carefully take his time to build a real home. Suddenly, as will often happen on clear sunny days, he had an idea.

He walked down the street toward the homes on the bluff, and spotted one that he'd previously called at, but no one had been there. Though the house wasn't ramshackle, it needed work. Some of the boards were missing on the side of the house, and a shutter hung off one of the windows. The gate was loose and rickety.

Obi fought his shyness and walked around to the back of the house. He knocked on the door and a middle-aged gentleman answered. He stood tall but was beginning to stoop a little. His thick, white hair touched his shoulders and his lips looked like a grim line etched in his face. He was like the house, Obi thought. Not totally broken down, but needing some work.

"Yes. What do you want?" he asked abruptly. "I have no work for you, no food and no money."

"Suh, I come here for my master."

"Your what?"

"My master, suh." It was all that Obi could do to not laugh as he watched the magical word change the man's attitude.

The lines in the man's face softened. "Your master?"

"Yes. I call him that. Just a habit, but I still serve him, because he always treat me right and I can't desert him in his time of need. His name be Mr. Booker and he send me to the paper to put in a ad for him. But he also said that I should go about and advertise for him some. Let people know that he's a master carpenter."

The man folded his arms and relaxed. "So you're his helper?"

"Yes, suh. Mr. Booker's been feeling poorly, that's why I can't leave him. It's me who do the work for him. He train me."

The man studied Obi carefully. "So you the one who's doing most of the work?"

"Yes, sir."

"But I'm paying Mr. Booker?"

"Yes, sir."

"But it's Mr. Booker who's the master carpenter. Not you."

"He train me."

"I don't know that. If I hire a master carpenter, that's what I want." He ran his fingers through his hair, and his brown eyes took on a mischievous glint, almost like a child. "Suppose I pay you directly. This business is between you and me. And what you give your master is between you and him. I can't pay you a master carpenter's salary. Three dollars to fix the gate, replace the spokes in the fence and the slats on the side of the house."

"That seem fair to me, but I have to use my master's tools," Obi said, surprised at himself for this tomfoolery. "So I have to give him the whole three dollars. If I'm gone out with his tools, then he know I have work. I'd be pleased to help you, but can't do it for three dollars." Obi paused and rubbed his forehead as though he were in deep thought. "Six dollars be good. I give him four and keep two for myself."

He studied Obi closely. "Five dollars. Three for your master and two for you. Be here first thing in the morning. What's your name?"

"Jennings," Obi said, "And your name, sir?"

"Richards. Master Richards."

Them the days done. You never hear me say master, less I talking about myself. "Yes, sir, be here first thing in the morning."

Obi rushed out of the yard before Richards saw him smile. He walked quickly back to Elenaville's main street, where he blended in nicely with the vendors and farmers and other black folk. He laughed to himself for the entire trek back to New Canaan. He had the work he wanted to do until the man caught on to him.

18

After the War we just wandered from place to place,
working for food and a place to stay.
—*DELICIA PATTERSON, FORMER SLAVE*

Obi was anxious to tell Rose what had happened. When he reached the cabin, Rose was cleaning her yard and the kitchen garden. Little Ray was underfoot and ran to Obi when he saw him. Obi picked him up and swooped him in the air. "How's Araba?"

"She seem much better, but I keeping her in the house. Grace is with her."

"Rose, I had to tell you this."

She wiped her forehead as she sat down on the porch. "This yard is a mess of work. What happen?"

He told her the story. "Now Obi, you shouldn't lie like that."

"Rose, that's the only way I can get work beside sharecropping. Anyway, he's robbing me. Ain't paying me a master carpenter's wage."

"You going to get found out."

"By that time he like my work too much to fire me. Rose, I mean to have my own business. Even if I have to act like I ain't me."

"You be careful. Sometime people get very angry when they been fooled by someone who they think don't have no sense." As they laughed, they saw a young couple walking down the path toward them.

"Good day," the man said when they entered the yard. "We looking for a Mr. Booker. The lady in the store say we find him here."

Obi's good cheer disappeared. He knew, even before they asked, what they wanted.

"Mister, we was told you could make a coffin for our son. But we can't pay you nothing now, sir. We don't even have a peck of corn, but we will pay later," the young man said.

Obi sighed. And wondered at the black telegraph on the island that had spread the news about him. The coffin maker. He wanted no parts of making another coffin. "How big was your baby?"

"Just a infant, one month," the young woman said tearfully.

"We sharecroppers. We pay you later. Give you a third of our crop," the man pleaded when Obi hesitated.

Obi shook his head. "It's not money. Why don't you make a simple pine box?" *Even Simon could do that.* "I have a lot of work here."

"I see what you made for another child. And we don't just want to throw our baby in a plain box, like he nothing."

The woman said in a soft, grief-stricken voice, "He was a lovely little boy, sir. You must have beauty in your hands, to make the coffins the way you do."

"We'll give you something, sir. We promise," the man added.

"Don't have to give me nothing. Come back at dusk." He pointed in the direction of Easter's land. "I'll be over there."

As they walked away, Obi made a mental note of everything that was still left to be done. Simon had only completed half of the foundation for the cabin, and logs still had to be cured and split. "Why didn't I tell them no?" he asked Rose.

"You have a good spirit. But you also riding a high and mighty horse, like Julius. I knew you was going to say yes when she start talking 'bout you have beauty in them big rusty hands. You need to go 'head and let Samuel and them other men help you finish that cabin so you and Easter have a place when you marry." She stood up.

Before he could respond, Samuel entered the yard. "Hey, Samuel,"
Rose chuckled, "we was just talking about you. Ain't this something?"
She sat down on the porch again. "How's Laura?"

"Better than me," he said, trying to joke. "Guess you wondering
why I ain't been around to help you, Obi."

"I was worried about you."

"Cain't sleep."

"You go on and help Obi, Sam. That'll make you sleep at night,"
Rose said. "He have plenty work for you."

"You doing fine without me, Obi. I can't do the work like you
nohow." Samuel looked weary.

"I have another task to do, and need you to work on the cabin if
you feel up to it."

"What about all the curing and notching and measuring and—"

Rose rolled her eyes in Obi's direction. "Some people too fussy for
me," she muttered.

"Help Simon prepare the tabby and then split some logs for me.
Can't make mistakes with that. I miss you, man. Ain't have nobody to
correct except Simon."

Samuel smiled slightly. They walked in silence to Obi's unfinished
cabin. Obi wanted to tell Samuel about how he'd tricked himself
into a job. The old Samuel would have bent over and laughed so
loud, birds would have scattered. Then he would have added his own
funny turn to Obi's story. But Obi understood. Samuel didn't need a
whole lot of talk and foolishness now. He needed a friend near him,
to wait quietly and patiently with him, for the healing time. When
they reached the property, Simon was already there, mixing sand and
oyster shells for the foundation. Obi concentrated on making the tiny
coffin.

Samuel intently and silently split logs. Just before dusk, when the
couple would come for the coffin, Obi sent Samuel home. "It be dark
soon, Samuel. You work hard today."

"See you tomorrow, Obi," Samuel said quietly. For the rest of the week Samuel quietly and faithfully worked on Obi's cabin, and Obi worked on Mr. Richards's property.

Obi had shored up the gate, replaced spokes on the fence, and made slats that perfectly matched the ones missing from the side of the house. By Friday he'd completed everything. Mr. Richards stepped out to the yard to do a final inspection and to pay Obi. Obi thought that Richards stood a little more erectly than he had at the beginning of the week.

He stepped around the yard with his hands clasped behind his back like a general inspecting his troops. Obi wondered whether Richards had been in the Confederate Army.

Richards shook his head, and at first Obi wasn't sure whether he was pleased or not. He shouldn't have any complaints, Obi thought, because he'd been closely watching him work all week.

"Jennings, your master taught you well. I don't think he could've done a better job himself." He took his billfolder out of his back pocket. "I'm giving you the five dollars I promised to pay. Was your master pleased with that?"

Obi nodded. "Very pleased."

"And I'm giving you an extra fifty cents for yourself. For the good work. That's for you, don't have to share that with your master." He winked at Obi.

"Now if I want you again, how can I find you? I saw your master's ad in the paper, by the way."

"You can write him, and he'll give me the message."

"New Canaan. What is it? Never heard of a New Canaan on the island."

"Used to be the Williams plantation."

"Oh, yes, I knew the family. Sold some of the land to their slaves. Lot of trouble there one time." He looked confused. "So New Canaan is a colored settlement?"

"Yes."

"What is your master doing living there? He's not a colored man, is he?"

"No, sir, he's renting the plantation house from the Williams family. He's not in the village. Just uses the general store to get his mail like everyone else."

"You'll hear from me again. I have a lot of work still, but I have to go to Beaufort. When I return, I'll contact you. Now you sure he was pleased with what I paid?"

"Yes."

"Okay then, because as good as your work is, you're still the helper. He's got to come out himself if he wants the full pay."

"Yes, sir," Obi said. "You have a pleasant evening." He knew Richards was suspicious and would eventually find out who Mr. Booker was, but in the meantime he'd made six dollars in one week, as opposed to six dollars a month for working as a field hand. He also knew that Richards was the kind of man who loved a bargain. He'd rather continue to do business with Jennings the helper than with Mr. Booker, the master carpenter.

It was not completely dark when Obi returned to New Canaan, so he went to see how Samuel and Simon were coming along with the cabin. As he approached, he was surprised to see that they'd completed the walls. He tried not to let his smile turn into a grimace when Simon spread his arms out and said, "Mr. Obi, you have a new home."

It was so small and crude. Obi could see every log and slat that was not perfectly straight. Some of the chinks between the logs were so large that a man's fist could fit through them. But they had done their best. And he would not have had this much completed if they hadn't worked on it. He reminded himself that it was temporary.

Obi took out his billfolder and handed Samuel two dollars. "Obi, I can't take money from you. No. Not after how you help me."

"Come on, Samuel. Take it."

"This ain't a job. It's helping a friend. That's how we do in the village. Tomorrow, some of the men coming to help us. We have that roof up by the end of the day."

"The work I was doing is finished. Y'all take a rest tomorrow and Sunday. I'll have time."

Samuel looked disappointed. "But I already told Brother Paul and James."

He sighed. "Okay, Samuel, y'all come on. We'll finish tomorrow."

As Simon began to clean some of the debris around the cabin, Obi handed him a dollar. "No, Mr. Obi, I can't take no money from you," he said, echoing Samuel. But Obi saw the longing in the boy's eyes. "You take it. This the first money you earn." Obi smiled. "It may be the last for a while. Don't waste it."

Simon's grin was wide. "Oh, thank you, Mr. Obi."

"Nobody was looking for coffins today?"

"No, sir."

"Maybe all this illness die down," Obi said.

He left Simon and walked to the store to see whether he had any mail. There was a letter from Easter. Obi was so happy to hear from her, he read it in the waning daylight before walking back to the cabin.

January 14, 1869

Dear Obi,

Excuse the long delay in writing. Do not think I have forgotten you. You are always on my mind and close to my heart. We have been so busy since Christmas and the New Year. The cold weather brings in more children. I am still attending classes in the morning and working in the orphanage in the afternoons and evenings and all day on the week-ends.

Obi, I was so sorry to hear about Charlotte's death. She was such a smart, happy, little girl. I cry each time I think of her. Please give Charlotte's mother and father my deepest sympathy. Unfortunately, many children fall sick this time of year. It is the same in the orphanage. There is so much illness among them.

I hope you and Rose and the children are all faring well. I think you had no choice but to keep the children, until you find them a good permanent home. It would have been cruel to just send them away to a camp. And Obi, I am so happy that you will give our "home" another chance. I don't think you will regret the decision. Life will bring many storms, Obi. But we are steadfast in our love. I'm counting the days until I return. Please keep yourself safe and sound. Give Rose my love.

I received a Christmas letter from Jason. He promises to write you for the new year.

Love, Your Easter

19

The poor little thing is only a few months old, and is suffering
dreadfully with whooping cough. It is pitiful to hear it moan.
—*CHARLOTTE FORTEN*, THE JOURNALS OF
CHARLOTTE FORTEN GRIMKE

When Obi entered the cabin, Araba didn't smile and throw her arms in the air so that Obi would pick her up. She barely raised her arms. Her cough was deep, as though her insides were hollowed out.

Sitting in the rocker, Grace held her.

"She has that whooping cough, I'm sure of it," Rose said. "I sent Little Ray and Scipio to stay with Melissa. The doctor give me some medicine. She wasn't so sick this morning." Rose bit her lips nervously. "Hardly had a fever."

"I'll stay here and help you tonight."

"No, you go on to the meeting. I send Simon for you if I need help. What happen with the work today, Obi?" Rose asked, trying to think of something else besides how sick Araba was.

He told her, and she said, "That man going to find you out."

"He's not coming here. Didn't you say they afraid to come in a colored village?"

"There's always one who ain't, Obi." Rose smiled.

Obi, Grace, and Rose took turns holding Araba, giving her small spoonfuls of broth and drops of the doctor's medicine. She was always enclosed in a pair of loving arms. When she opened her eyes, she had a familiar and loving face to gaze on. Obi held her, and she was as light as a whisper. *Come on, little Araba. Get up and fight this thing like you fight to walk.* She opened her eyes as if she'd heard his thoughts. Araba looked at Obi, smiled sweetly and passed away quietly in his arms. Araba was buried the following night, in a coffin he'd crafted. He carved a heart on the lid and inside the heart etched *Araba Booker a loving daughter.* After the funeral, Obi wrote to Easter.

February 1, 1869

Dear Easter,

I hope that you are fine. Unfortunately, once again I have sad news to tell. Araba, one of the children that Rose and I been caring for, died, and was buried tonight. I made her coffin and it was the most sorrowful work. All of New Canaan came to her funeral, even Miss Fortune and Julius. I am worried about Grace. Her eyes are dead again. She left this world with her sister.

This is a joyless, hopeless place Easter. It's killing the children. I should have put that little girl on the transport and let her go. Maybe she'd be alive now. There be too many people here troubled in mind and body.

Julius talks about land, and the land association, but I see no land up for sale. I cannot make a decent living here, much less build a business. I had to make believe I was a fool who hardly knew slavery over, just to get a piece of carpentry work. It seems as though I have become the village coffin maker. The money I saved from the army is fast going. People here have nothing and no hope of getting anything. They losing the land they had and most of them have to sharecrop. They never make enough money to buy a piece of land.

But I will wait for you as I promise. The cabin is almost com-

plete, though it is small and plain. I think of Araba and the way
she always get up everytime she fall. So I will get up and continue,
but I am afraid for us Easter. It seems everytime I begin to find a
little peace, something terrible happen. How much time do we have,
Easter? I long to be with you before something else happens again.

Your Obi

Obi was tired to the bone as he walked down the shelled road the evening after Araba's burial. A ferry had come in, and he wanted to see whether he had any mail. He'd been up since dawn, working on the cabin. He and Samuel both, working hard and quietly all day—both men fighting off the painful memories, the disappointments.

He breathed in the spicy smell of Miss Mary's store. The storm hadn't changed that, but it had added a thick crack down the wall behind her counter. Several other customers were in the store, and he was surprised that they all greeted him warmly, by name. "Hello, Mr. Obi."

"Sorry about your little girl."

"Mr. Obi, thank you for what you done for us," one woman said softly.

Obi remembered her. The last mother he'd made a coffin for.

"It's nothing, ma'am."

"I was sorry to hear about your little girl," she added.

"Thank you. I hope you and your husband faring well. Miss Mary, I have any mail?"

"Yes. I think you do," she said, putting the mail basket on the counter. "Think I saw an envelope that look like it had your name on it."

Obi found the envelope, but the handwriting was unfamiliar, and almost childish. He quickly opened it and scanned the chicken-scratch handwriting for a signature. Jason Jennings. While Miss Mary and the other customers talked, he sat down on a crate and read the letter.

Jan. 5, 1869

Dear Obi,

    Happy New Year. I hope you is fine, Obi. Well it nice to hear from you after all of these many years. Easter tole me you find Rose and all of them people. Is Rose still fat and bossy? She also tole me that you an her is getting marry. Well that's nice. You all will be happy. I know Easter can't see no one but you. I know she be thinking of you when the sun rise and still thinking about you when it set.

    It be nice for us to live together like we did on the farm, but I ain't never coming down there to live again. As long as there be a stage somewhere for me to sing and dance on, you never catch me up in nobody's cotton patch. I'm not talking big on myself, but the people here in Chicargo love the way I sing, dance and play the banjo too. I learn to play the banjo so good I could make a big yam foot like yours do a jig. (ha, ha, ha) Can't pull my ears now like you used to do. So I guess you better disabuse yourself of any thought of me coming back there. I still don't no the words that would make you no how sad I was when you and Easter leave me. You has to be inside my heart to no how bad I feel at that time. It make me sick. I remember it still and it still hurts to think on it.

    But Easter loves me and come back for me. You didn't. I older now and understan. You was getting free and couldn't take no little pissy tail boy like me with you. So you must understan how I feels. I find freedom too. Right here in sweet Chicargo. We be here for another month. Next we head for New York City and I been tole that's even better than Chicargo. I also hear some of the people talking about maybe we go to London. Maybe I sing and dance for the Queen. I with the Georgia Minstrels, that's our group. All of us be colored.

Well Obi, the show start soon so I have to go. Maybe one of these days you and Easter come and see me in a show. When we go to New York, I will send Easter my address and she can give it to you. Can't wear out my fingers with all of this writing, have to save them for pluckin that banjo. (ha, ha, ha)

Save a space for me in your house for when I visit. I come and visit when Easter returns and you all get hitched. Bye Obi.

Love, Jason Jennings

Obi shook his head as he read the letter. *That boy still a rascal and a jack-a-behind.* He didn't like the sound of Jason's letter, and was reminded of performers he'd seen who came around the army campsites. Most of them were beggars and vagabonds.

"Mr. Obi," Miss Mary interrupted his thoughts. "Hope that wasn't no bad news make you look so sad."

"No. Not bad news. Just news."

"Mister Obi, I want to tell you, you help so many people during these bad times making all them baby coffins. All a body had to do was to ask you, and you did it."

"Thank you." Her words were useful to him at that moment. He gazed at the wall behind her again. "Miss Mary, that wall ready to fall down around your head. I fix it for you next week."

She leaned on the counter. "Now Mr. Obi, I was going to ask you about that. This time I paying you for your work."

"I'll take care of it for you." As he walked along the shelled road, he wondered what kind of rude boy Jason had become.

When Obi entered the cabin, the memory of illness and death and Araba weighed on him. Grace sat silently in the rocker, her face buried in her sister's blue blanket. Scipio squeezed next to her, fast asleep. Simon put the plates on the table, and Rose stirred a pot of grits, while Little Ray, whining and whimpering, clung to her skirt.

"What's wrong with Ray?" Obi asked, picking the child up, hoping that he wasn't ill.

Rose lowered her voice. "He keeps asking for 'Aba.' " Rose looked at Grace sadly and then at Obi and shook her head. "Grace, you put that blanket down and come sit here with us."

Grace didn't move.

"Araba with Jesus now. You going to make yourself sick. Come and eat," Rose insisted.

As Obi listened to Rose, he remembered the feelings he didn't even have words for when he was taken from his mother. "Rose, leave her be. She'll eat later."

Rose sighed and sat down at the table.

"You need to take a rest yourself. You look tired, Rose."

"I be okay tomorrow. Me and Grace clean this whole cabin thoroughly. Air it out too. Get all that sickness out of here."

"Rose, why don't you let Little Ray stay with Melissa for a few days longer? Get some rest."

Obi knew Rose was tired when she agreed with him so easily. "Maybe I do that. Then me and Grace can work on that kitchen garden too."

"Don't do any work tomorrow. Rest."

He told Rose that Jason had written to him. "He doing fine," was all Obi said. "Singing and dancing."

"That's the only thing that rascal know how to do," Rose said, appearing to be too weary to think about Jason or anything else.

Obi answered Jason's letter later on that evening.

February 2, 1868

Dear Jason,

I was happy to receive your letter and know you are fine. I am also happy that you enjoy your life in the minstrel shows, but you know that is not a decent life. Many of those show people end up beggars and vagrants in the street. I am sorry that I had to leave you. I was young and thinking only of myself. You and Easter are my family. Easter wants to stay here in South Carolina. I am not so sure, I am just waiting for her, then we want you with us. I know you will say that I didn't want you when I left the farm. Again, I am sorry for that. But there is nothing I can do, as the people here say, them the days done. That's the past. We have a future to look forward to. Easter worries about you, and I do too. It's a hard life you're in. You don't have to be a farmer. I don't want to be one either. Nor does Easter. But we want you with us. You need to come to be with people who love you, Jason.

Another thing, Jason. When I see you I'm boxing you between the ears good. You ain't too old for that. I know I still bigger than you. I show you what a big yam foot I have. And that wasn't a nice thing you said about Rose. She is a good friend and was helpful to you too. Write me back soon and think about what I say.

Love, Obi

20

To everything there is a season. . . .
A time to keep silence,
and a time to speak.

—*ECCLESIASTES*

On Sunday morning Obi planned to finish off his cabin. He woke up before everyone else, took a refreshing bath in the creek, and returned to Rose's for tea and grits. All that was left to do was to whitewash the walls, make the shutters, and put in the floors. At least he would have real floors, no dirt floor.

When he returned to the cabin, Grace sat in the rocker, her face buried in Araba's blanket.

"We all going to church. I think that make us feel better," Rose said to the top of Grace's head.

Little Ray and Scipio were scrubbed clean and ready for church, though Scipio was quiet and Little Ray continued to ask for "Aba."

"Grace, leave the rocker," Rose ordered.

Grace had turned to stone.

"Grace, Grace," Obi called to her. He clasped her shoulders and shook her gently, as though waking a sleeping child. "Grace, come on, stop that. Mind Miss Rose."

Slowly she raised her head, and for no reason that he could comprehend, Obi thought about how he and Buka used to fish on Sunday mornings.

"Grace, we going fishing."

"Fishing?" Rose wondered whether she'd heard correctly. "Did you say fishing? They have to go to Sunday school and church."

"God be everywhere."

She rolled her eyes at him. "Fishing too?"

"Maybe." He lowered his voice so that it was barely audible. "I use to fish with Buka on Sundays, and it made me happy."

She shook her head. "That old African never really give up his heathenish ways, Obi. And he almost make a heathen out of you. Best let that child come with me. She needs God's love."

"It ain't go hurt her this one time." He took Grace's hand. "Come, we find a bucket and we make two hand lines. You ever been fishing before?"

She shook her head.

"You'll like it."

"I going to pray for you, Obi," Rose said as he and Grace walked out of the door.

The morning was clear and bright. A perfect day for fishing. So they sat by the creek, Grace wiggling her toes in the water. He didn't have to tell her to be quiet.

He handed her the line. "See, this is how you hold it. Very still, and the fish will bite."

"Can I just keep my feet in the water? I like to look at the water."

The first time she ever say she like anything. "Why you like the water?"

"They ain't no trees in the water."

"Trees?" He frowned as he watched her stare at the water. He understood.

"Grace, trees can't hurt you, not unless they fall on you. Don't think about them awful times."

When Obi caught a squirming catfish, Grace glanced and then looked away. "Maybe the people wriggle like that when they get hang in the tree."

"Grace, that's over now. We have a good fish dinner tonight."

She let it be. The morning passed slowly and peacefully. He looked at the position of the sun and rightly guessed that it was about two o'clock. He felt almost as good as he used to feel when he fished with Buka.

But when they returned home and Obi saw Melissa brewing a big pot of soup and several of the other village women leaving the cabin, he knew that something was wrong.

"What happen?" he asked, rushing inside.

"Rose took ill in church. Simon at my cabin with the two boys. Them two little ones can stay with me till she get better," Melissa said. "She just have the chills is all. That bad weather and then taking care of the sick child. I think she just need a day or two of rest." She eyed the bucket. "Look like them fish been biting."

"Yes. You take some, since you have the boys there. Send Simon back here."

"Don't worry, Obi, Rose be strong. She had a touch of malaria last year. Just overwork herself."

Obi checked on Rose. "I tell you to rest. You always trying to do too much."

"I'll be fine, Obi. Just caught a chill is all." She sat up in her bed and took the bowl of soup Grace handed her. "Same thing happen to me this time last year. Melissa make such a fuss, just because she see me shivering some in church. It's still dampish."

"I'm sending Simon to find that doctor who work with Miss Fortune."

"Obi, that ain't necessary. Let the doctor alone. She have real sick people to tend to. Have her running over here for nothing," Rose complained.

"There was men in my regiment who catch malaria and the doctor give them quinine and knock it right out of them."

"You bad as Melissa."

When Simon came back from Melissa's, Obi sent him to find the doctor. He returned in a short time. "Miss Fortune say the doctor's away. Won't be back till tomorrow, maybe." Simon looked worried. "Mr. Obi, Aunt Rose be okay?"

Obi wondered when "Miss Rose" had become "Aunt Rose."

"She'll be fine. Don't you worry." *This start as a peaceful day.*

Obi and Simon cleaned the fish, and he made a fire outside the cabin and put the skillet over the fire, frying the fish the way he and Buka used to do. Grace made a big bowl of grits to eat with the fish. Rose insisted on getting out of bed and eating with them. "You all making too much of a fuss." She tried to eat heartily. "Obi, you sure know how to fry some fish."

He could tell that she wasn't really hungry and was forcing down the food.

"Tomorrow I begin to plow over some of them field."

"Is you mad, Rose? You need to rest another day. And this weather never settle so early. Simon help you when he come in from school."

"I feel fine by tomorrow."

"Don't you know what the word rest mean?"

"I too poor to know what rest mean."

"If I see you outside, I running you back in the house."

Rose tried to laugh heartily. "You go on, Obi. Turning into an old woman, like Melissa."

The following afternoon, however, Obi didn't have to worry about Rose not resting. As he and Samuel mixed sand and oyster shell to fill in the chinks between the logs, he saw Simon running toward him.

"My Lord, what happen now?" Obi said.

"Aunt Rose be too sick," Simon gasped.

21

For Death is a simple thing
And he go from door to door
And he knock down some, and he cripple up some
And he leave some here to pray

—*SPIRITUAL*

"Why Simon send for you? I told Grace to make me some tea. Just caught a chill is all," Rose said, her hands shaking as she picked up the tin cup. She wore her field dress, and her head was wrapped in a blue kerchief.

"You said that yesterday, Rose. I'm sending Simon to see if the doctor return yet, or maybe Miss Mary or Melissa have some quinine. Rose, go back to bed. You can't work in no field today."

Grace looked frightened as Rose shuffled to the bedroom.

"I staying around to help. You go on outside and work on the garden," he ordered Grace. She needed air and light, Obi thought. Maybe if she were outside, the warm sun and growing life around her would keep her mind away from thoughts of death.

"Can I stay in, sir, and help Aunt Rose? Can't see so good outside."

Now Grace too was calling her "Aunt Rose." He wondered which one of the children started that. "But you saw good in the water."

"I know, Mr. Obi."

"You help Miss Rose, then. No sitting in that rocker, grieving over Araba. She's in a good place, Grace. With your mama, you understand?"

"Yes, Mr. Obi."

Simon returned an hour later with a large bowl of soup sent by Melissa and the news that the doctor had not yet returned from Beaufort. "Miss Mary say she don't have no quinine, but she'll pull up some roots for you. She say to come to the store this afternoon."

All day long, villagers stopped by to see "how she faring," taking a moment from their own fields and kitchens. Virginia, Anna, and Isabel visited Rose, bringing herbs, teas, and prayers. After their work, Samuel, James, and some of the other men dropped in to see "how Miss Rose be." And Miss Fortune also walked down the shelled road to call on Miss Rose.

Even Julius made a quick visit on his way to a meeting on the other side of the island. "I going to help the people start a Republican club and tell them about the work we're doing on the Land Commission," he informed Obi.

Rose insisted on sitting at the table and eating dinner with them. "I feeling much better now," she said. But Obi knew better. Her eyes appeared cloudy and weak, and her hands trembled slightly as she put a spoonful of broth to her lips.

After everyone went to sleep for the night, Obi sat at the table and wrote Easter.

February 5, 1869

Dear Easter,

I hope that you are fine. I do not think you have yet received the letter I wrote to you a few days ago. Except for missing you, I am okay, but I can't say the same for everyone else. Rose doesn't feel too well. She would be fine if she stop overworking. The next time you write send a message to her to stop pushing herself the way she do. She want to plant cotton again, but if she does, she'll kill herself for sure. The fields will take all the life out of her. She won't make any money.

I heard from Jason, but I do not like the sound of him. I think he is running wild in the streets. I will save the letter to show you.

The cabin is almost finished. I think in the end, Easter, it will only be a temporary shelter for us. I am beginning to feel that New Canaan is a cursed place. I am waiting impatiently for your return.

Your Obi

The following morning, when Obi checked on Rose, she breathed heavily, and her quilt was drenched. She'd gone from chills to a fever. She needed a doctor. He touched her forehead, and it was on fire.

Obi walked over to Miss Mary's store. "Mr. Booker, I was expecting you yesterday." She pulled a large sack from under the counter, containing her store of roots and herbs. "Mr. Booker, you take and boil this here tania root and add two teaspoonfuls of mustard and a spoonful of vinegar."

He dug in his pocket. "How much I owe you."

"Mr. Booker, I could never sell you a thing. Not after what you done for me." She looked at the wall that Obi had shored up for her.

He left Easter's letter with Miss Mary for the mail pickup on Friday and then walked to the school to find Miss Fortune and let her know how sick Rose was.

The doctor finally arrived that evening. Obi and Simon sat at the table, waiting for her to complete her examination. Grace sat in the rocker, held Araba's blanket, and stared into space. Obi wondered whether she even remembered how happy she had been on Sunday. When the doctor walked out of the bedroom, she motioned to Obi to step outside. "She has recurring malarial fever. But I think she can fight it off." The doctor handed Obi a vial of medicine. "This will help her. She needs rest."

"I hope you tell her that."

"I did."

Obi thanked the doctor for coming and offered to pay her. "No charge. We do this work through the missionary society. Miss Fortune told me about you, but I haven't had the chance to meet you and personally thank you for putting up the school for us."

The next morning Obi stayed near the cabin so that he could be there until Simon came home from school. He let Simon plow the ground that Rose used for her kitchen garden. "You don't go nowhere, Simon," Obi warned him. "And you call me if Miss Rose take a turn for the worse. I'm working on my cabin."

Obi worked alone now. Samuel and the other men had to plow and prepare their fields for spring planting. Obi didn't mind. He could take his time and do things the way they were supposed to be done. Once he had a piece of wood in his hands, carefully curing it over the fire and cutting and smoothing it, he forgot sometimes that this was supposed to be a temporary cabin, built by the men of New Canaan. Not the home he'd planned, made lovingly by his own hands.

As he worked, he dreaded two things during those solitary February afternoons—Simon running to him, announcing Rose's death, and having to make another child's coffin. Neither occurred. Dr. Emmy returned with more medicine and a hopeful prognosis. "She's basically strong, and has a will to fight this. I think she'll recover." For the rest of the month, Rose's life seemed to hang on an invisible thread, woven from prayers, Melissa's broth, the doctor's medicine, the people who loved her.

On the last Sunday in February Obi stayed in the house to look after Rose and decided to send Simon and Grace to Sunday school, because he knew Rose would want that.

"Mr. Booker, you don't want some help 'round here? Want me to help you make them slats for the floor in here?" Simon asked. "Remember you was saying Aunt Rose's floor need fixing?"

"No, you and Grace go to Sunday school."

Simon didn't look very happy. "Yes, sir."

"Don't you want to see Scipio and Little Ray?"

"They going to cry to come back home with us."

"I know. But they still be happy to see you and Grace. Go on out to the pump and clean yourself."

"Yes, sir," Simon mumbled.

When Grace came out of the bedroom with Rose's bowl, half filled with broth, he said, "Grace, you and Simon go on to church and Sunday school. I'll watch Aunt Rose." *Got me saying it too.*

"We not going fishing, Mr. Obi?"

Obi was surprised. He had thought that the fishing meant little to her. She'd never asked him about going again since the first time. "You liked fishing?"

"Yes, sir."

"After y'all come from Sunday school, then we'll go."

He saw her eyes begin to cloud over and stare, and then she bowed her head. "I like the water, sir."

Obi smiled to himself. *Maybe the old African was right. God be everywhere.* Now he and Grace had their own Sunday routine. "Grace, you see if Aunt Rose need anything else. We'll go fishing when Simon come back from Sunday school."

Obi walked outside with Simon before he sent him off, explaining, "Grace say she can't see so well. So I let her stay home."

Simon seemed relieved. "It all right. She ain't going to do nothing but sit and stare no way. Then the other kids laugh at her."

"I hope you ain't laughing along with them."

"No, sir."

The women came after church to help out and sit with Rose awhile.

Simon went outside to get the fishing lines, and Obi had to disappoint him again. He recalled that the few times anyone else fished with him and Buka, it wasn't the same. He tried to explain it to Simon. "Grace has seen a lot of sorrow. Her mind is troubled. She likes the water. It seems to help her mind some."

Simon's long thin face dropped. "Yes, sir."

"I need you to be here in case something happen to Rose so you can call me. By the time them women talk, and cry and wail, it be tomorrow before anyone let me know anything."

"Yes, sir," Simon repeated.

Obi was sorry. Simon wasn't in a much better condition than Grace, but at least his mind was all in one piece. "We'll go fishing together when Aunt Rose get better," Obi promised.

Grace and Obi walked to the river and sat at the bank, Grace wiggling her toes in the water. Obi's mind drifted. Since his and Easter's cabin was so small, he might build a separate kitchen. He wondered whether Mr. Richards would ever contact him again. When Rose was better, he'd go to Elenaville again.

Obi felt a tug on the line. When he glanced at the opposite side of the creek, he saw Simon racing toward them. His heart pulled and wrenched in his chest. The death watch was over. Obi wished that Simon would slow his pace some. He didn't want to hear the message. Why was God so hard on them? Simon could barely talk, but Obi thought he saw traces of a smile. *This fool boy gone mad.*

"Mr. Obi . . . Mr. Obi . . . Mr. Obi, Miss Easter here!"

22

Thou art the soul of a summer's day,
Thou art the breath of the rose.
—*PAUL LAURENCE DUNBAR*

"What?" Obi dropped his line in the water, and the fish swam away, line and all.

"Miss Easter . . . the lady who write you."

Obi scrambled off the grass before he fell in the water too. "You sure? You ain't making some mistake?"

"That's what the lady say, Mr. Obi."

"Come on, Grace." He pulled her up, and they raced back to the cabin. Obi practically crashed into the back room like a wild man. There she was. Easter. Sitting on the edge of the bed, leaning over Rose. Two other women stood around the bed. When Obi saw her, he wanted to gather her up in his arms. "Easter?" he asked, as though he still didn't believe his eyes.

She stood up, and he wondered for a moment whether he was dreaming. Was this stylish young woman in a maroon traveling suit with a short jacket and long skirt and a small maroon hat to match, was this young woman his little Easter? *No more a girl in a homespun dress.* The last time he saw her she was wearing dusty trousers, and her hair was cut short like a boy's. But she had had the same smooth, deep brown skin, heart-shaped face, and full mouth that he saw before him.

At first he was too shy and ashamed to hold her, sweaty and rough as he was. But she was *his* Easter.

"Easter," he murmured huskily. "My Easter?" They embraced and kissed, and he held her to him tightly. Then, embarrassed, he became aware of the women smiling at them and Grace staring at the floor. He hadn't realized that she'd followed him into the room.

Obi introduced her to Easter.

"Hello, ma'am," she said shyly.

"Come on child, you stay with us." One of the women took Easter's place on the edge of the bed and motioned for Grace to sit next to her. "Mr. Obi and Miss Easter have to talk."

His arm still around Easter's waist, Obi kissed her forehead and led her into the main room. Simon still stood at the door. "Mr. Obi, can I go fish now?"

"Go on. There's another line in the bucket. Make sure you catch something."

They sat down at the table, across from one another, and Easter began to cry. She wiped her eyes and tried to control herself, but couldn't. "Obi, I'm sorry. I can't believe I'm finally seeing you again after all these years." She reached across the table and rubbed his smooth face. *Even more handsome. Mature.* She lowered her voice. "And Rose, she's so sick."

"Maybe she get better now that you here," Obi said clasping her soft hands in his rough, callused ones.

"So silly, crying like a baby. After you told me that Charlotte and the little girl you and Rose cared for died, and then when you wrote me and Miss Fortune wrote me about Rose, I had to come home. I had to be here with you. To help you. Obi, I had so much to do before I left, I didn't have time to even answer your letters."

She sounded just like Miss Fortune, he thought. *She learn Yankee speech well.* It was strange, though, coming out of her mouth.

Her eyes welled up again. "I hate to see Rose like this. She's so thin and weak."

"Seeing you help her along."

She nodded. "I hope so."

There was so much he wanted to say. He didn't know where to begin, so he said what was foremost on his mind. "You home to stay, Easter?" He thought he felt her hand twitch.

"Yes. Until Rose gets better, then I . . ."

Grace entered the room. "Ma'am, Aunt Rose want you."

He watched Easter walk away from him and noticed her carpetbag sitting next to the rocker near the fireplace. Obi was nervous, agitated, excited, pacing the small cabin, feeling as though he were in a box as he listened to the murmur of the women's voices. Hardly believing that Easter was here. Her voice, soft, smooth, wafted from the bedroom. He didn't know what to do with himself, so he rummaged through the box where he kept his stationery. He removed Jason's letter so that he could read it to Easter.

Easter walked out of the room wearing her old homespun dress— the same kind of dress she used to wear when they lived at the Jennings farm.

"Now you look like my Easter. How is Rose?"

"She's feverish still. The women are going to make her some broth."

"Too many of them in there. Going to suck up all she air."

"Obi, you're the same, yes? Still don't like to have a lot of crowd around you."

"Let me show you the cabin," Obi said.

"Our cabin," Easter corrected him.

They walked along the narrow footpath that led to their future home.

"I always remembered how pretty the island is, Obi. I miss it so."

"A lot of the trees come down in the storm."

"Not all. There's enough left, Obi. You can hardly tell there was a storm. I really missed the moss hanging from the trees." She gazed at the trees, the sky, as if seeing all of it for the first time. "There is still snow in Pennsylvania," she said. "Here it feels like spring."

"Well, here it is." He studied her face closely. She smiled, but Obi doubted that it was a true smile. He thought he saw disappointment in her eyes as he imagined how small the cabin must look compared to the Fortune's home in Philadelphia.

"It's lovely, Obi. It really is."

He didn't believe her, and with Easter standing next to him, the cabin looked even smaller and cruder.

"It's not what you been used to living in up North."

"I've been living in someone else's home. This be my home." When she laughed, her eyes curled exactly the way he remembered.

"Now you sound right again. Like one of us. Easter, the house I was building for us was going to have a porch all around it so that we could look out at the sunset and at Rose's cabin and fields."

"Obi, even in this little cabin we can see Rose's fields."

"Yes. All the trees blow down."

"It's just how you look at it, Obi." She clasped her hands. "You know we can plant fruit trees. And you can put a fence around the property, and I'll plant flowers around it."

"You always liked flowers. You know what I was thinking too. Building a separate kitchen."

"Obi, this is fine the way it is." She looked inside. "Just need some furniture."

"Maybe I'll add another room. We have a bedroom, with a bed, Easter. I know you ain't like sleeping on a pallet on the floor again."

"You sound more hopeful than your letters."

"Because you're back here with me." Obi tried to be diplomatic, but he didn't know how. "Easter, let us marry. We can go to the magistrate tomorrow."

"I have to go back and finish school and work a few months more."

They sat on the dirt floor and leaned against the wall. He put his arm around her, and she rested her head on his shoulder.

"You don't want to marry?"

"I do, but not before I finish what I started." She paused and stared at him. "I told them that I would return to Philadelphia as soon as Rose is better, and I'll make up the time I've been away."

"So if you stay here a month, instead of returning in May you come back in June?"

She nodded.

"Easter, I don't want you to go back. I want you here with me."

"I said my plan was to go back, Obi. But when I see you—I don't know what to do."

"We should get married, Easter. That's all you need to do."

For the first time in eight years she felt whole. Away from him all of those years, she had been separated from a part of herself. "Obi, we will find our way. Figure out what's best to do."

"I find my way. We marry, and I take care of you. That's what's best to do."

Easter listened to the cries of the seabirds. Obi's arms were strong around her, as they'd always been. Even when she was a child.

Obi dug in his pocket. "Jason found his way. I thought he'd be with us." He pulled the letter out of his pocket. "Read this letter from him."

"Big yam foot?" She threw her head back and laughed.

"I don't think that's funny," he mumbled.

"He's angry with you, but he still loves you. He was angry with me when I went back to the plantation for him."

"We need to go up there and get him when Rose is better."

"Jason wouldn't stay down here. And we can't make him. He's not a child anymore. He's right, you know. You took your freedom, and now he's taking his."

"You got him before."

"That was different. He was a child then. I wanted to free him. Now that I freed him, I can't put him back in chains."

"I've seen them show people. Many of them be beggars and vagabonds."

"All we can do is love him and pray for him. Whenever I write him, I tell him not to forget who his people are. Some people take the long way home, don't you know." She stood up and pulled him off the ground. "This feel like when we used to sneak and have those picnics, remember?" She giggled.

"I don't want you to leave, Easter."

"Obi, when I left to come here, I had to see you. When you write and tell me Rose is sick and the children are dead, I had to come home to help you, see you." She squeezed his hand. "When I'm near you like this, right here with you, I feel like I never want to part from your side again. But my plan was to leave when Rose gets better."

"You could teach here."

"Then I couldn't marry at all. I told you that in my letter. Female teachers working for the society must be unmarried. But I could run my own private school."

"I need to begin a life too. I need a wife and a family, and I'm not waiting another eight years. If you leave, then I leave too."

"I told you, there's no decent work in Philadelphia."

"I'd go to the West, where there's land. I tired hearing about land for sale here. I ain't seen none yet. You could meet me there when you finish with school."

He recognized the familiar frown lines that always appeared on her forehead when she was upset. "I want us to stay here, not in the West. New Canaan is our home."

"Then don't leave."

"Obi, my head is spinning. Right now we have to see about Rose, you know. Remember, Obi, you left me and Jason. You went across the river."

"You didn't want to come with me, Easter," he said angrily.

"That's past. God make it so that we're back together."

"And you making it so that we separate again," he retorted.

"Obi, can't you understand how I feel?" she pleaded. "When you left me in the camp, I understood why you left."

He put his arms around her as the shadows deepened outside the cabin.

"I'm not arguing with you. I just don't want you to leave. That's all. But I'll try to understand."

"We're together now. That's what's important."

"But for how long?"

"Until Rose is well."

"Suppose she never gets well," he said.

"I feel deep inside me that she will." Her voice cracked slightly.

Obi wished he could be as sure as Easter.

"I guess we better go back now, and see about Rose," Easter said.

Before they left, Obi gazed around the cabin. "Me and Simon can sleep in here tonight," he said. "So you can have some privacy."

"I'll make a pallet in Rose's room. I don't want to disrupt you and the boy."

"You used to sleeping in a bed."

She put her arm in his as they walked down the footpath toward Rose's cabin.

"I'm so tired, Obi, I could sleep in a cow pasture. You haven't finished the floor or put in a window yet in the cabin. I'll be fine in Rose's room."

"I've slept on the bare ground and under the sky when I was in the army. And Simon, that boy can sleep anywhere. I'll put a piece of tarpaulin up to the window."

After living in the big city and a big house, he wondered whether she already felt as though she were in a cow pasture. What would happen to them? Eight years apart. They were no longer the same people.

23

The heart of a woman goes forth with the dawn,
As a lone bird, soft winging, so restlessly on,
Afar o'er life's turrets and vales does it roam
In the wake of those echoes the heart calls home.
—*GEORGIA DOUGLASS JOHNSON*

March 1869

In the week following Easter's return, she cared for Rose as best she could and puzzled over Grace, who politely did everything Easter ordered her to do, saying, "Yes ma'am, no ma'am," but when she had no chores, would still sit in the rocker and hold Araba's blanket. Easter knew from her own work at the orphanage that she should not impose herself on the child but wait for Grace.

Obi tried not to think about Easter leaving or Rose dying. He meticulously completed putting in the cabin floors and the shutters on the windows. When Samuel saw the floor, he said, "Man, you have to build a whole new house around this fancy floor."

Every afternoon that week Easter and Obi spent a few moments alone, sitting together inside the cabin for only a short spell and, as Obi said, "Learning each other again."

They leaned against the wall, his arm around her, her head on his shoulder, just as they'd sat together the first time he showed her the cabin. They tried to close the chasm of eight years spent apart. They told one another their stories.

And on a rainy Friday afternoon, as they sat inside the cabin listening to a gentle spring shower, they finished talking about the past and had to face the present and an uncertain future.

"I know you don't think much of New Canaan, but you helped many people, especially Rose. If you weren't here, what would have happened to her?"

"The villagers would've helped her. You know that."

"But not the way you helped. And the children, Obi. You surely helped them."

"One is dead, no help there. And the girl and boy latch themselves to me for no reason."

"Araba's life was short. You and Rose made it sweet in the end."

"That little girl never stayed down once she learned how to walk, you know. She keep getting up no matter how many times she fell," Obi said. He leaned back on the wall and closed his eyes and smiled as a simple truth was revealed to him. Araba was the messenger. Life knocks you down, but you keep getting back up.

Easter gave him something else to think about. "Children know. They know who loves them and who will harm them," she said.

He rubbed her back tenderly. "Where you learn that? In them schoolbooks?"

"I saw it in the orphanage. Children know."

He was quiet a moment, enjoying the faint scent of rosewater from her hair and the back of her ears. "You love that work, don't you?"

She nodded.

"I know you don't belong in no field, behind a plow. You ain't no farmer's wife. And I ain't no farmer."

"You understand how I feel then?"

"Yes, but I still want you to stay."

"Will you understand if I go back North?"

"You want me to smile and say, Yes, Easter, I happy for you and I want you to go North? I will understand. I will wait for you. But I won't be happy about it. People dropping dead around us like flies. All we have is this time. We don't know nothing about tomorrow. No matter what happens, Easter, I have to keep pulling myself up is all."

"Tomorrow is God's will, not ours."

"Leaving me is *your* will, not God's."

She said nothing. Just kept her head on his shoulder. He'll wait, she thought. I will hurry back. One day he'll truly understand.

After Easter went back to the cabin, he continued working. He was going to surprise her with a fine table—their first piece of furniture. He'd try to complete it before she left. He adjusted the rack of boards he'd made and lit a small fire under them. He picked up a long, thick piece of wood, placing it over the rack.

Suddenly, a familiar voice startled him. "Jennings, I want to see you too. When I asked for you at the store the lady said she didn't know you. But I'd find Mr. Booker here." His sharp eyes peered around the yard and at Obi's cabin.

Obi nodded. This white man surprised him. Walking so deep inside a colored village. "Hello, sir."

"You think your master let you give me a couple of months? Where is he?" Richards eyes darted nervously. "I'll pay you twenty-five dollars a month." He lowered his voice. "I'll tell your master I'm paying you less. You can keep something extra for yourself." His eyes swept the yard again. "So, where is Mr. Booker?"

Obi stared at him. Unsmiling. Silent. He sensed that Mr. Richards was uneasy and suspicious despite his bold trek into New Canaan by himself. "He's not here. What do you need to see him for?"

He looked annoyed. "I like to meet the people I do business with."

"You're doing business with me."

"Who are you?"

"Mr. Booker."

The man turned several shades of red before he spoke. "What?"

"I said, I am Mr. Booker. Obidiah Booker."

"How dare you make a fool out of me?" he thundered. "I knew something wasn't right about you."

"I didn't make a fool out of you. You was ready to throw me out as soon as I entered your yard, sir! I did good work, and you only pay a helper's salary."

"You misrepresented yourself to me. You lied."

"It was business. I'm a artisan. You ain't finding no one 'round here better than me. You got a lot of work for a little bit of money. And you know it."

Richards, red and angry, turned around as though he were walking away, then stopped and faced Obi again. "You are an arrogant scoundrel."

"I was a slave. Had good teachers," Obi snapped. *This man know he still want me to do the work.* "What you want done, sir?"

"This puts things in a different light. I thought you were the helper."

"I ain't do nothing to you but give you good and proper labor. And I want to be paid by the job, not by the month."

Richards took his watch out of his pocket. "I have to think about this again. I can't trust you."

Obi walked back toward the rack of wood. "Write me at the general store when you make up your mind. Good day, sir."

Obi didn't go to the Republican Club in the evening. He didn't want to miss a moment with Easter. As he sat in Rose's cabin, watching Easter set the table, Obi felt complete. He told her about Richards.

"Wish I was there to see his face," Easter chuckled. "You think he'll hire you?"

"I know he will, because he likes my work. Figures he can pay me less than he would a white carpenter. I have to charge him less, just to get the work, but not much less."

She handed him a spoon and sat next to him on the bench. "You should charge more for the beautiful work you do."

Easter glanced at Grace sitting in the rocker and staring, as always. But the blanket was neatly folded on her lap instead of buried in her face. Easter wondered whether there was some meaning in that. "Grace, give Aunt Rose a cup of tea. Then we'll eat."

"Yes, ma'am," Grace said.

When Grace left the room, Easter stopped setting out the plates and sat across from Obi at the table. She lowered her voice. "I have a message for you from Miss Fortune, Obi. She said that Grace could be sent to the Boston School for the Blind, and there is an opening at the Orphan House in Boston for her brother."

"They would be separated."

"I know. I told her that you wanted them to stay together. She said that both schools are excellent and they are in the same city."

"I think they should be in the same school and the same home. And Grace ain't blind."

"I know that too. But maybe something is wrong, and her vision comes and goes. Miss Fortune said she'll speak to you tomorrow when she comes to visit Rose." She paused a moment. "I almost forgot to tell you. Julius left a message for you today."

"Julius know where I was. He could bring me the message himself."

"He also wanted to find out how Rose was."

"And how you was," he mumbled.

She rolled her eyes at him. "You're jealous of Julius? What's wrong with you, Obi? We all been knowing one another since we ragtail children."

"What's the message?"

"The Land Commission is selling land around here for a dollar twenty-five an acre to heads of households."

Obi sucked his teeth. "That man know I ain't no head of no household. So what's he coming to me with a message like that for? Just want to slip in here and see you."

Grace walked back in the room.

Easter quickly got up from the bench. "What happened, Grace? Rose finished her tea so soon?"

"Ma'am, she say she want some real food. She hungry."

Easter hugged her. "Oh, Grace. Aunt Rose is getting better," she said excitedly and dashed into the bedroom.

Instead of sitting in the rocker, Grace asked, "Mr. Obi, want me to finish setting the table?"

"Yes, that's good."

"Is Aunt Rose getting better?" she asked, echoing Easter.

"I hope so, Grace."

Obi sent Simon for Dr. Emmy.

24

I take my way down [the] street and stop at
every house, giving medicine.

—LETTERS AND DIARY OF LAURA M. TOWNE

"I think that the disease has run its course," Dr. Emmy said, touching Rose's forehead. "Don't you try to do too much, your body is in a weakened state."

"That's what I tell her, doctor," Obi said. "She always try to do too much."

"You all worry me too much. I want to see my son and Scipio too."

Easter brushed back Rose's matted hair with her hand.

"We'll bring them home tomorrow," Easter assured her.

Rose ate a small bowl of grits and two biscuits and kept all of it down. After they'd all eaten and Rose was sleeping comfortably, Easter and Grace cleaned the plates while Obi helped Simon chop firewood. As Easter hung the skillet over the fireplace, she watched Grace sweeping the floor. When will this little girl recover? She wondered.

Easter walked over to her, gently took the broom out of her hands, and leaned it against the wall. "Grace, do you know how to write your name?" she asked, remembering the magic and power she had felt when Rayford taught her how to write her name.

Grace shook her head.

"Let me show you then."

While Easter took her writing supplies out of her carpetbag, Obi and Simon returned to the cabin with armloads of firewood. Obi was surprised to see Grace sitting at the table instead of in the rocking chair.

Easter winked at him as he sat on the bench opposite Grace. "Well, Miss Easter, what're you doing now?" he asked.

"You'll see," she said, sliding next to Grace on the bench. She wrote Grace's name on a piece of paper. "That's how your name looks, Grace. Can you see your name?"

She nodded.

"Let's write another name. How about Araba's name?"

"Yes, ma'am."

"Now, this is your brother's name," Easter said. "Scipio."

"Ma'am, how you write Miss Emma, Mr. George, and—"

Obi interrupted. "Grace, stop that. I told you to forget all that."

Easter hushed him. "She can't forget. They're locked inside of her." She turned her attention to Grace again. "We'll write those names too. You tell me what they are."

As Grace called the names, Easter patiently wrote them down—all twenty-three people who had been hanged. For the rest of the evening, Grace and Easter were absorbed in names.

Easter stood up. "You better rest now, Grace. Tomorrow is another day. I'll show you how to write the letters." Grace walked into the bedroom. She left Araba's blanket folded neatly on the chair.

Easter sat down next to Obi on the bench. She lowered her voice, and he could hardly hear her over Simon's snoring. He'd passed out on Easter's pallet. "That little girl isn't blind or mad. It's the thing she witnessed. Perhaps writing those names down help get the evil of what she saw out of her. I've seen children like her in the orphanage."

166   Joyce Hansen

"I didn't think she was blind," Obi said. "Just don't want to see."
He took Easter's hands in his. "Well, when you leaving us, Easter?
Rose getting well now."

"She still needs help."

"Maybe Grace getting well too. She ain't blind. Could be a big
help to Rose."

"I'll leave when Rose can do everything she use to do, Obi. We
talked about this already. And when I finish my work in Philadelphia,
I coming back."

He smiled to himself. Whenever she was upset she lapsed into their
island dialect. *Forget she Yankee talk now.*

"That little girl needs to be in school. Miss Fortune told me the
boy is one of the brightest children she's ever taught. I believe Grace
is the same. I wager I could teach her to read in a month or two."

"You staying that long?"

"I'll write to Philadelphia after Rose regains her strength. She's all
skin and bones now."

He kissed her hands, and while he held them near his lips, his
usually somber eyes gleamed playfully. "You can leave tomorrow, Easter. Between me and Grace and Simon and the rest of the village, we
can take care of Rosie."

She pulled her hands away from him. "Obi, this no time for jokes.
Rose is still not herself."

He gave her a long good-night kiss. "Girl, I think your feet stick-
ing in this sandy soil."

When Obi stepped out of his cabin the following morning, the
jasmine bushes colored the fields gold. It seemed as though they had
blossomed overnight. He noticed for the first time a cluster of bushes
covered with white blossoms behind the cabin. As he started to go
back inside to wake Simon, he saw Miss Fortune, holding a parasol
over her head, stepping lightly down the narrow footpath. She appeared as bright and pretty as the morning.

"Good morning, Miss Fortune."

"Mr. Obi, I'm sorry to disturb you so early like this, but I had to tell you the good news before I left for Beaufort this morning."

Obi looked a little embarrassed as he gazed around the yard. He couldn't have her sit on a log or on the floor of the cabin as he and Easter did. "Ma'am, I'm sorry I don't have a speck of furniture in that cabin to invite you inside."

She smiled and waved her hand. "Oh, Mr. Booker, that's quite all right. I can't stay long. But I wanted to tell you this since I will be away all of next week. Easter told me that you didn't want to separate the children. I understand that. There is a school for orphan colored children in New York that will take both children. If Grace is blind, she'll get help there, for they have a school for the blind as well."

She smiled and caught her breath. "Now, that's one choice, Mr. Booker. The other choice is a childless couple who have just bought land on Pleasant Point. They will take in both children. The husband is a printer and will apprentice the boy. And Grace, well, the wife can train her in the domestic arts."

"Where this couple from?"

"They're from Boston and have moved down here."

"Are they colored, ma'am?"

"Why, Mr. Booker, what difference does that make? Do you want these children to have a decent home? These people come from one of the finest northern abolitionist families."

Obi was fascinated at the way Miss Fortune was almost turning red. He didn't realize that some colored people turned red when they were angry too.

"Mr. Booker, do you want these children to have a decent home or not?"

"New York is too far away. And the white people up there already burn down a home for colored orphans. And as for the Boston people,

I don't think Grace would like to live with a white family. I think she be too afraid of white people because of what happen to her."

"Mr. Booker, it's been my experience that children do not see color. They love whoever loves them." She stared at him for a moment. "I don't think you'll find *any* home good enough for *your* children."

Obi shifted his weight uncomfortably from one foot to the other. He didn't want her to think that he was ungrateful. "Miss Fortune, I appreciate everything you done. I'll think about it, and then let you know soon as you get back from Beaufort."

"As you wish, Mr. Booker. But remember, it's not easy to find a good situation for children nowadays. I'll call on Easter and Miss Rose, and then I'll be on my way."

"Thank you, Miss Fortune, for all of your kindness." He appreciated her help, but he was not letting them go unless the situation was fit and proper.

Scipio and Little Ray returned home that evening. Ray looked shyly at his mother at first, taking tentative steps toward her when he entered her room. Rose, sitting up in bed, smiled and said, "Come on, baby." He recognized her voice and her smile and ran to her.

Scipio stood quietly in the corner until Rose called him to her as well. "You well now, Aunt Rose?" he asked.

"Much better, baby."

Scipio showed off for Easter, letting her see how well he could read. Grace reviewed the names Easter had written the night before. Easter knew that Grace wasn't truly reading. The names were already deeply embedded in her mind. But after reciting her sad litany of names, Grace asked, "Miss Easter, how you write Naomi?"

"Who is Naomi?"

"My ma. I want to see how her name look."

"I'll show you. Yes, you should know your mother's name," Easter said as she carefully wrote and recited the letters. Obi wasn't sure, but he thought it was good that she was thinking about names other than the people she'd seen lynched.

Little Ray sat next to Scipio at first, looking wide-eyed at Scipio's book and Easter's sweet face, and then falling asleep on Scipio's shoulders. And Simon, snoring loudly, stretched out on Easter's pallet. Obi wished this time would last forever.

When Obi left that night, Easter stepped outside of the cabin with him. The bright stars reminded her of the time she'd run away alone from the Confederate camp. They had been just as bright. "I want to tell you something, Obi."

"Easter, you know I want to say something to you too. I been troubled all evening. Since you leaving, it's best not let those children get too used to you."

She folded her arms across her chest and tilted her head to one side. "You let them grow accustomed to you. That little boy thinks his last name be Booker."

"You mean *is* Booker," he corrected her.

"Don't correct me. I know what I'm saying." She lowered her voice. "I have some talk for you, Mr. Obi. Miss Fortune told me you're fussy about who gets the children. Why don't *you* keep them? Then you'd be head of household and could buy that land cheap."

"I'm not keeping them children just to get land. I'm surprised at you, Easter, for thinking such a thing." He stared at her as though he were watching a stranger. "That's what you learn up in the North? How to make use of people?"

"But you ain't letting them go, so you may as well make use of them. They already made use of you." She smiled as though she knew something that Obi didn't. "Grace's little spirit is healing. She's safe and someday she may even be happy. Obi, you know I'm not telling you to take those children just to get some land. "

His temples throbbed. "You know, Easter, I'm tired of all of this. I should've just gone with my friends out West. Maybe they was right." He pointed his finger in her face. "You're leaving me and now telling me what to do about them children."

"They love you, Obi," she said calmly and quietly.

He held her by the shoulders and shouted, "Do *you* love me?"

"Why you wake the whole neighborhood?" She folded her arms again. "I would have liked to return to Philadelphia and finish school and work at the orphanage a spell longer. I don't ever want to do field work, unless I'm starving. And that cabin, Obi, does seem small after the house I lived in up North."

"I know it all the time. Why you wait till now to tell me that? Why you even come back here?" His voice was rising again. "Rose get better without—"

She covered his angry mouth with her soft hand and continued.

"And I had a hard time getting accustomed to sleeping on a floor again. But freedom would be bitter without you, Obi. And we do have an orphanage here already, don't we?"

"What're you saying?"

"Don't you un—"

He waved her away. "I'm tired of all of this."

Easter looked exasperated. "Would you listen to me? I am saying that I will *not* go back to Philadelphia. I will stay here and marry you, and we will raise Grace and Scipio and open our own orphanage. You could build another cabin and a schoolhouse. Rose could be the cook for the orphanage. You could teach the boys the carpentry trade, and the bigger children could farm for the orphanage to earn their keep. We could take in children whose parents have to work on other islands, and charge them a fee. Buy the land that's being sold. If we get more land, then we could rent some of it for income and have the big boys and girls work the rest of it for food. Those are some of the things we did in Pennsylvania." She stopped to catch her breath. "Some of the northern missionary societies could help us too."

Obi stared at her, his mouth slightly open, not knowing how to easily move from anger to understanding.

Her eyes curled into a smile. "Obi, you know you can't send those children away. And there's more children on this island who need help. We need an orphanage right here. We will call it the Jennings-Booker Home for Colored Orphans. We'll even have enough room to keep that space for Jason."

He struggled through her torrent of words and tried to get to the point. "Easter, you staying here and marrying me?"

Her slender arms encircled his waist. "Obi, the work is here, and my heart is here with you."

25

The very oaks are greener clad,
The waters brighter smile;
Oh, never shone a day so glad
On sweet St. Helena's Isle.
—*JOHN GREENLEAF WHITTIER*

May 1869

"You think this day ever come, Obi?" Samuel asked as he brushed Obi's jacket, making sure there was not a speck of dust or lint on his new suit.

Obi pulled on his shiny new boots. "Samuel, these only the second pair of boots I ever own in my life."

"And the army give you the first pair and they wasn't even new." Samuel laughed loudly and happily as if this were *his* wedding day.

"You know the money I spend on this suit? I could buy lumber for an addition to that rickety cabin you and Simon build for me and Easter." Obi smiled, making sure that the crease in his trouser leg was sharp.

"You have that big job in Elenaville. I know the man is paying you well. You could hire a work gang throw that house up for you in a day," Samuel joked.

"Richards cry about every two cents he pay me."

"You only get marry one time." Samuel fingered one of the sleeves on Obi's jacket. "This good material. You can use this same suit for your funeral too."

"This a one-time suit then, eh?" Obi laughed.

Samuel stepped back and studied him. "I do believe Easter is going to fall in love with you all over again." He patted Obi on his back. "Well now, sir, you is finely turned out and ready to jump that broom." Suddenly, Samuel looked very serious. "That's a blessed thing you doing. Keeping them children. I never tell you this, but one time I asked my wife about taking them since our Charlotte was gone home." His voice cracked. "She say no, 'cause Charlotte was a free-born child, and them children still have the stink of slavery on them." He brushed the back of his hand across his eyes. "Man, this your wedding day. Why I conjure that up?"

Obi patted Samuel on the shoulder. "I understand how she feel. We all have it. But in time we clean it off."

The door flew open without warning. A tall, rail-thin young man in a white linen suit and a white felt hat practically danced into the cabin. His grin was wide and bright, and he grabbed and hugged Obi. "Is them old yam feet going to dance a reel for your wedding?"

Obi was speechless for a moment. "Jason?" He gave him a bear hug and then held him at arm's length. He could not believe it. He'd become a sharp, snappy city boy. Obi hugged him again. "I am so happy to see you. Easter told me she wrote you. You seen her yet?"

"Oh, yes. She say, hurry. She tired of waiting. I met them children you all adopted too. That poor little boy don't know what a hard time he's in for." Jason grinned and then turned to Samuel, shaking his hand. "How you doing, man?"

"Hey, boy. You come back down here in the briar patch with us?"

"Not to stay. Going back to Chicargo tomorrow before Obi put a plow in my hands."

Samuel's laughter and Jason's bright excitement filled the cabin.

"You know, Jason, I could still box you behind the ears," Obi chuckled as they left the cabin.

Almost all traces of the storm had disappeared. Two of the azalea bushes had come back to life. Violets bloomed along the footpath to Rose's yard, and the blackberry bush behind the cabin was covered with white blossoms.

When Obi, Samuel, and Jason entered Rose's yard, everyone congratulated Obi and welcomed Jason. Jason rubbed his hands together, "Obi, I going to dance my fool head off for you and Easter."

The yard was transformed. The children had decorated the gate and fence with garlands created with moss, pink azaleas, and violets. Two tables covered with white tablecloths stood near the fence. The aroma of fish stew and gumbo floated to them from the cauldrons in the backyard.

Brother Paul directed Obi to stand under a brush arbor. It had become a New Canaan tradition among the original settlers to marry under a brush arbor reminiscent of slavery days, when they had to worship outdoors and in secret. "So we don't forget where we come from," Rose had explained to Obi.

Rose walked out of the cabin. Though she was not as plump as she had been before her illness, her great eyes were large and beautiful. Julius graciously held out his hand to help her step down from the porch, and it occurred to Obi that maybe Julius was beginning to cock his eyes on Rose.

Grace followed Rose out of the cabin. Her hair was neatly braided, with a big blue bow on one side of her head to match the blue dress trimmed in white lace that Obi had bought her. She did not stare into space but seemed startled at the sight of so many people smiling in her direction. "My Lord, look at that child. Don't look like the same little girl," Miss Mary whispered to Samuel's wife.

Obi motioned for Grace, Scipio, and Jason to stand near him.

When Easter stepped out behind Grace, there was first a murmur and then clapping. She wore a plain white cotton dress trimmed in lace, with a sprig of tiny white flowers in her hair. Obi could not stop smiling at his bride as Easter took her place next to him.

Jason, standing directly behind Obi, whispered in his ear. "It do feel good to be home."

Epilogue

January 1, 1871

Dear Thomas,

Happy Emancipation Day to you my friend. I was so pleased to receive your recent letter and to know that you and Peter are buying land in Dunlap, Kansas. It's been so long since the first letter you wrote to me, I began to think that you all were lost in the Plains. Or, that you never left New Orleans. Well, boys, no need to save any of that Kansas land for me, my feet are stuck in this sandy Carolina soil. I have even purchased twenty acres of it. So many things have happened since we last saw one another.

My Easter and I were married over a year ago. I own a carpenter's shop and keep busy enough. We have begun to build a small orphanage and school. Remember those children we found hiding in the woods? They followed me here to Santa Elena, and Easter and I are raising two of them as our own. Sadly, the youngest girl died back in '69. But Thomas, the greatest news is that Easter has given me a wonderful Christmas gift. Last month she gave birth to a beautiful baby girl. We have named her Araba. She is the joy of our lives. I have never been so content.

Now, let me tell you how all of these things came about . . .

JUN 9 08	DATE DUE		

F
HAN

Hansen, Joyce.

The heart calls home

PS 309
SCHOOL LIBRARY

644078 01440 01123D 02295F   001

P. S. 309 B'KLYN.
LIBRARY